MW01136475

MARY TING

MICHAEL'S JOURNEY

HALO CITY

THE CROSSROADS SAGA

This is a work of fiction. Names, characters, places, and incidents are products of the author's imagination or are used fictitiously and are not to be construed as real. Any resemblance to actual events, locations, organizations, or persons, living or dead, is entirely coincidental.
Copyright © Mary Ting 2013

Licensing Notes
All rights reserved. No part of this book may be used or reproduced in any manner whatsoever without written permission, except in the case of brief quotations embodied in articles and reviews.

IMAGINARIUM
BOOK FESTIVAL

To the readers at Imaginarium Book Festival.

Thank you so much for attending and supporting all the authors. I want you to know that it means the world to me. There is no book world without the readers. I appreciate you all.

If you would like to be part of my ARC group, please reach out and I'll give you a link. You can also check out the social links listed on the last page.

AND ask me about Crown of Wings and Thorns story game. I can't wait for you to read this book.

Thank you so much from the bottom of my heart. Enjoy Halo City, novella, and teasers from my other fantasy series.

Hugs,

Mary Ting/M. Clarke

soulful, spellbinding stories that excite the imagination.

Chapter 1
Michael

Desperation squeezed my heart. I lay on something soft, and I needed to wake up, needed to know where I was. As my mind and body started to sync, I blinked and finally got a clear vision of white walls and an empty room. The bed under me was the only furniture.

Sunlight surrounded me. I raised my hand to block the rays beaming through the window. The light shimmered like gold glitter on my hand, and I felt no warmth from it. *Strange.*

Pain hit me hard in the rib cage as if I'd been struck by a sword. I dropped my hand and curled into a ball until the ache subsided, then I carefully pushed myself to a sitting position. I glanced down at what I wore—a white T-shirt and white, loose-fitting pants. Had someone changed me? Why was I there? What happened?

Searching through my memories gave me answers. Dantanian had tried to kill me. He had run me through with a sword, the reason for my pain and why I hadn't healed already. But he had struck Trinity too. She was either badly wounded or— I couldn't bear the thought of the alternative.

1

If I didn't try to find her, the guilt of leaving her behind would tear me apart. She *had* to be alive. And where was Aden? That was the strangest part of my memory. I remembered our blades connecting as we lunged toward each other, but the reason behind it was hazy.

Aden loved and cared for me like a son. Why would he try to kill me? My memories were unclear, and nothing made sense. As I tried to recall more of my past, it only frustrated me. The guilt of killing countless innocents consumed me. Regret burdened my heart, and it felt heavier than anything I'd endured before.

I cautiously swung my legs over the side of the bed and touched my bare feet to the cold floor. My knees buckled and I planted my hand on the mattress to keep from falling. My stiff legs would take a while to get used to moving again. After slipping into my shoes, I dragged my feet across the floor to the window, but I couldn't see anything but the bright light. So I headed toward the door in hopes of finding answers on the other side.

Footsteps approached. I pressed my back against the wall and looked for any weapon. I had no idea if I was in a friendly or hostile environment. Unable to find anything, I readied my fists in front of my chest.

As my pulse quickened, I worried who would enter. Without any weapon, I would rely on my strength, but I didn't know how much energy I could muster. The footsteps stopped, the doorknob turned, and three teenagers crept in.

When they didn't see me on the bed, they turned simultaneously and saw me standing like a statue. Loud yells startled me, so I echoed the sound back at them. After the noise ended and silence resumed, we stared at each other until finally the female, who had long brunette hair and the face of an angel, cleared her throat.

"Hi," she said sweetly. "My name is Vivian."

"I'm Caleb." The first guy smiled. He had a friendly, innocent face.

The guy who had not introduced himself paced back and forth, studying me. Then he stood with his arms crossed, tilting his head back as if trying to intimidate me. He was going to get on my nerves.

"Sooo, you're Michael," he said.

"It depends on who's asking," I huffed, mirroring his challenging expression.

"I'm asking." He pointed to himself.

Not the answer I'd expected.

"And you are?" I asked, narrowing my eyes at him.

"They call me Davin." He moved closer to me, piercing his gaze into mine. "I'll be keeping my eye on you, so you'd better not do anything a Fallen would do."

"Davin." Vivian smacked his arm. "You don't say that to our guest." She turned to me. "Sorry. He can be—well, you'll get to know him. Anyway, welcome to Halo City or Crossroads, whichever you prefer."

"Halo City? Crossroads?" I asked out loud. I stumbled back a few steps and used the wall for support. The bright light that gave no warmth made sense now, but I still couldn't imagine how in Heaven's name I'd gotten there.

"You okay?" Caleb asked.

"Yeah, I just need a minute." I covered my face with my palms. Gathering myself, I looked at the angels in front of me and wondered if they were Alkins or something else.

"Do you remember anything?" Vivian asked, looking concerned.

I wasn't about to share any personal information with strangers. "Look, don't take this the wrong way. I need to speak to your leader or superior, or whatever you call the master."

Vivian smiled. "We're the officers in Halo City. We're here to help you in any way that's necessary. And Agnes will be stopping by soon to check up on you."

I walked to the bed, trying to hide the pain that struck me again when I sat down.

"You're still healing." Vivian reached out her hand, then lowered it.

"I'm fine." I curled my body inward to lessen the ache.

I wasn't fine though, and it wasn't just the pain. It was all of it—being there, not remembering much of anything, and being with these angels I didn't care for. Wondering how long they would stay, I was just about to risk being rude by asking them to give me some space when Vivian spoke again.

"We'll be on our way. We just came by to introduce ourselves."

"It was good to meet you." Caleb smiled.

He smiled too much. Why did he have to smile at me? What one good thing did I ever do for him? I should have responded to be polite, but I just looked at him until Davin broke my gaze.

"Like I said before, I'll be watching you, Fallen." Davin tried to give me a threatening look, but it came off as kind of goofy looking.

His eyebrows furrowed together and his lips pursed like he was going to blow me a kiss. If I had been in a better mood I might have laughed, but not that day.

Instead of offering a comeback, I raised my brows as if to challenge him. Vivian did what I wanted to do. She gave Davin a solid clout on the shoulder. Good for her.

When they left, three other angels walked in, each smiling. They were different—sophisticated and majestic.

"Hello, Michael. My name is Phillip, and this is Agnes and Margaret." He gestured to them. "We are angels called the Divine Elders. We are God's angels, created after the

Royal Council was formed. We are beneath the Royal Council and above the Alkins, who are half human and half angel. The familiar term would be *Nephilim*. Halo City is only occupied by the Alkins."

I raked my hair back and sighed. "I'm not sure why I'm here."

I felt baffled at the revelation, but frankly, I didn't care. I just wanted to get out of there and find Trinity.

"You are an Alkin, Michael," Margaret said. "You don't remember. Aden got to a large group of Nephilim and convinced them to side with him. A battle occurred during the process when we were supposed to take you, but a group of you rebelled. Had we known Aden would betray us, we would have gotten to you sooner. We apologize for that."

"I don't understand why you're apologizing to me. I should be begging for your forgiveness. I was the one who went against the angels of light." I lowered my head, expressing my humility. Bending my knee, I tried to kneel, but I had to stop midway from the pain.

"You're still healing." Agnes gripped my arms and helped me to stand. "Why didn't you tell me? I can help make it bearable."

"No—" The word came out louder than I had intended. "I-I'm sorry. I didn't mean to—"

"It's okay. We know this is difficult for you." Agnes patted my shoulder. "You should feel better tomorrow. The Alkin officers will take you to your room when it's ready. We've made a special place for you."

"I'm—I'm not ..." I almost said I wasn't staying, but I closed my mouth.

"We'll be on our way so you can get your rest," Phillip said. "We'll talk again later."

With a unified smile, they left.

Chapter 2

I stood by the window and stared at the light glistening on my hand. How strange I couldn't see what was on the other side besides the bright light.

The sun never set in Halo City. Distinguishing how many days had passed was impossible.

As Agnes had predicted, I felt much better, almost myself. Unfortunately, it didn't mend my guilt. I didn't want to be there—or anywhere else. I would have preferred my life to have been taken during the battle.

I had to sneak out of this room if at all possible. My main dilemma was not knowing what awaited me or who had been assigned to keep an eye on me. I would be cautious of me, too. After all, I was once a Fallen who couldn't be trusted.

Agnes had mentioned something about me having my own room. Although a sense of belonging appealed to me, and their warm gesture touched me deeply, I couldn't stay. There was nothing for me in Halo City.

A soft knock interrupted my thoughts. "Come in." I stood up in case one of the Divine Elders had decided to pay me a visit.

Vivian entered. "Hello, Michael. May we come in?"

Caleb entered next. "Hello, Michael."

I didn't have a chance to reply. The door swung wider and Davin barged in.

"Well, looks like you're doing much better." Davin's voice was too loud. "You're actually taller now that you can stand up straight."

Vivian nudged Davin and gave him the evil eye, then she flashed a smile at me, and said, "We're here to take you to your room."

I followed them out. Everywhere we turned there was that same bright light, penetrating through the walls and soothing me. Davin walked behind me, breathing down my back. If it wasn't for Vivian and Caleb, smiling at me as we continued down the hall, I would have punched Davin's face. That would send him a clear message to back away.

After rounding the corner, we entered a room.

"Welcome to your place." Vivian waved her hand outward.

The setup was similar to the other room, except I could see the trees and flowers out the window, and a bed was set against the back wall.

"Don't worry." Vivian walked toward the window. "No one can see you from the other side. Agnes thought you would prefer this room since it gives you a nice view of the fountain and the garden."

"Thanks." I smiled. I was astonished to see kids running around the fountain, so I rolled in with my questions. "How many children?"

"I can't give you a specific number, but you're only seeing about half," Vivian replied.

"How many of *you* are there?" I asked.

"Countless," Davin said quickly, his tone stern. He pointed a finger at me. "So don't think about doing anything stupid."

"Davin." Vivian lightly smacked his arm. "Don't be like that."

"What?" Davin shrugged. "I'm just saying."

Caleb gaped between them, then looked at me. "If you'd like to visit the garden, we can take you."

I turned my attention to the children laughing and running. They looked so happy. Why couldn't I feel that way? But then again, I deserved all the pain and suffering for what I'd done. No amount of grief could make up for my past wrongdoings.

Beyond them, the fountain sparkled as if the sun's rays shone on crystals. I was mesmerized for a brief moment until Caleb called my name.

My lips twitched, a hint of a grin. "Thanks, but … I think I'd like to be alone for a bit."

"Sure. We understand," Caleb said.

"When you're ready, we'll show you around," Vivian said sweetly.

"Yeah, just don't wander around by yourself." Davin used that same stern tone again.

I wished I could give him a good punch to put myself in a better mood, but I had to use restraint.

Showing my violent side would not be good so early on.

I didn't know how many days had passed, but I stayed locked up in my room of my own free will. I didn't want to see or talk to anyone.

Agnes came by to check on my wound. I didn't mind her visits, but I did mind Davin. Every day he asked me when I was going to come out of my room. I told him to go away and leave me alone, but my words seemed to go in one of his ears and out the other.

Often I heard Vivian, Caleb, and Davin whispering about me behind the doors. They didn't know I had a heightened sense of hearing, so they didn't know I listened in on a lot of their conversations.

"Don't go in there," Vivian whispered. "He'll come out when he's ready. If you annoy the heck out of him, he'll never want to leave the room. I mean, I wouldn't want to come out if I knew you were waiting for *me*."

"Yeah, I'd have to agree with Vivian," Caleb said.

"Well … that's I-I don't … fine. Okay," Davin stuttered.

"Don't you remember when the Divine Elders took us?" Vivian said. "Many of us were afraid. We needed time to adjust, time to heal and to forget, and time to move on. Michael needs his space right now."

Davin sighed. "Okay, okay. I get the point. I remember. I did move on quickly though."

"But not everyone is like you, Davin," Caleb said. "You're a social butterfly. You made friends with everyone and helped them through the hard times with your funny ways."

"Funny?" Davin sounded offended. "I hardly call it funny. I think of it as more like … a talent." His tone was arrogant.

Vivian scoffed. "Yeah, whatever. Anyway, I'm headed toward the main hall, and you're coming with me."

"Who's going to make me?" Davin said.

Davin yelped in pain, and I imagined Vivian tugging him away by his hair or ear. I had to admit, I'd enjoyed that conversation. When a small puff of air seeped out of my mouth, I realized it was a little chuckle. A tiny one, but it felt good.

My laugh was a little ray of sunshine peeping through the ominous clouds, only to hide again.

Chapter 3

Many days had passed, but I wasn't sure how many. It didn't matter. I was determined to leave, and it was time to make my move.

I exited my room and stealthily walked down the hall, listening for any footsteps. I didn't know where I was going, but I ended up in the center of a foyer with a high ceiling. Despite the absence of windows, the golden light filled the room, filtering through the crystalline walls.

I paced toward the grand double doors and they magically opened. What I saw next took my breath away—a blanket of puffy clouds extending around me like an ocean. The sight gave me the purest sense of serenity. I'd swallowed a "Heaven" drug, and the happy, peaceful feeling filled me completely. I was in a state of euphoria, and I didn't want to let it go. I'd heard of Halo City, but I'd never imagined it to be so grand and beautiful.

A massive golden light, resembling an angel's halo, circled the vicinity. Now I understood why the Fallen couldn't pass through. The light was a shield. But I had passed through. I pondered this thought for a minute. Surely, I needed to do something for penance. Had my past sins been forgiven?

None of these things mattered. I had to find a way to get out, and I refocused on the reason—to find Trinity. She had been wounded trying to save me. I needed to help her. With no sense of direction, I opened my wings and flew. The view was even more breathtaking from above.

The wind caressed my face as I soared alone. Glancing behind me, I saw the place where I had stood a second before. It looked like a castle, the largest I'd ever seen—not that I'd seen many—and built from crystals. As I soared without a destination, I followed my instincts.

Planting my feet on the ground, I gazed at the field of tall grass that seemed strangely out of place. It stretched without an apparent end. Not knowing what lay on the other side stopped me from dashing through, so I decided to take a peek.

I pushed my hand through the reeds, but they wouldn't budge. They were stronger than me. I paced to another section and tried again, but again the grass didn't budge. That grass had to be my exit, an exit that would not cooperate.

I was a prisoner. How was I going to explain to the Divine Elders what I had been trying to do when I was forced to go back?

I prepared to use every ounce of my strength for one last try at pulling the grass apart when a mocking voice said, "I dare you to try it."

Completely surprised to hear Davin's voice, I did what I knew best — attack. With a quick turn, I swung my legs beneath his feet. When he dropped to the ground, I straddled him and my hands went to his throat.

"Hi. Surprise," Davin's choked voice was even more annoying. "You're finally out of your room."

"Did you follow me?" I gritted the words through my teeth. It would have been the perfect opportunity to choke the life out of him, but I wasn't a killer.

"You want to get off me, or did I just make your dreams come true by letting you get on top of me?"

I knew he was trying to lighten things up, but I wasn't in the mood. In fact, I was never in the mood to even be in the same room with Davin. He was something else. With a frustrated grunt, I jolted up. I should have offered my hand, but I didn't feel like being polite.

"What was that for?" Davin stood up and rubbed his neck. "Nice move with the foot, but I didn't deserve that."

"Don't be a wimp. You think that hurts? Haven't you been in a battle before?"

"No, I haven't. And for your information, I'm really good with my sword, but the Divine Elders believe we're not ready. Anyway, what are you doing here?"

I turned my back to him. "It's none of your business."

Davin made a funny sound, the same sound I made when I was irritated. "Excuse me for what you may think is 'none of my business,' but everything that happens here is my business. So, buddy …"Davin poked me in the arm since I wouldn't look at him. "… I'll ask you again, why are you here?"

My fist balled up tightly as I tried to restrain it from sending it into his face. "Listen …" I poked him back in the chest as I focused my eyes on his. "First of all, I'm not your buddy. Second, I don't belong here. Third, I don't like you."

Davin took a second to process all my words. He blinked and his eyes told me I had said something to offend him. His droopy expression softened my heart. I hated that he could make me feel bad for what I'd said. But his reply and his somber tone made it worse.

"You think you're the only one who had it bad? All the Alkins, including those you didn't get to meet yet—and believe me, there are tons of us—had no choice. We were taken and forced to be here. They wiped out all memories of our past. No memories of our parents, brothers or sisters, or what kind of life we lived. Everything is gone. So while you got the chance to roam on Earth with Aden and live the life you think you wanted, all of us were here, trying to cope, trying to understand and to make things work. We didn't rebel. We didn't sulk or complain. We just coped. We believed in the forces we couldn't see and tried to find the purpose of our existence."

After hearing his words, I knew he was a better being than I could ever be—a thousandfold. The right thing for me to do was apologize, but my pride got in the way, so I said nothing and stared at the grass.

"You can't get through it." Davin slapped the grass. "But I can. I'm the gatekeeper."

The word gatekeeper rang in my head. It sounded familiar. Had Aden informed me about them?

"Gatekeeper," I repeated.

"Yup. Several of us are gatekeepers. We can let in and out those we want."

I furrowed my brow. "Sooo, you can let me out?"

"Yup." Davin gave me that funny look he'd mastered, between serious and humorous.

At his goofy expression, my lips curled just enough to hint at a grin, but I wasn't going to give him one. If I had been in a better mood, I would have laughed.

"But I'm not going to," he continued.

He annoyed the heck out of me. "Really?" I stood tall in front of him. "I can make you." My tone was low and harsh. Flashing my wings with a snap, I purposely fanned them out to intimidate him.

"Holy Moses!" Davin jumped back with his fists ready to attack. "What in Heaven's name are those? They're bigger than ... wait, you don't scare me."

Without another word, he bolted into the grass. Though I knew it would be impossible for me to do the same, I tried nonetheless. That section of grass felt different. I pushed through, but not all the way.

Davin's movements were odd, like he was attempting to do some kind of a dance or jump awkwardly.

He rambled out loud, "You think you're hot stuff. I dare you to come get me. I'll even let you have the first punch. What are you, chicken?"

Davin flapped his arms and clucked like a chicken. Boy, this one was a nutcase. But what really got me was when he stuck out his tongue at me. I didn't

15

know why, but he had pulled the last patient string I had left. I punched through the barrier, gripped his arms, and lifted him up effortlessly from the back of his shirt.

Davin froze, looking utterly shocked as his feet dangled. "How did you do that?" he asked in a squeaky tone.

I let go and watched him fall to his knees. While he dusted off his pants, my feet shuffled on pebbled ground. It was like day and night. Clouds on one side and dirt on the other.

"Where are we?" I mumbled under my breath as I gazed at the endless dirt road and the tall grass that hid the other side.

"We call this place Crossroads. Sometimes lost souls wander through here. We don't know why or how, but Margaret guides them out when she senses their presence. I believe these souls were not prepared to move on from their present life. Perhaps they lost their lives abruptly and didn't get a chance to say goodbye to their loved ones. Or perhaps they're scared to find what awaits them on the other side. Whatever the reason may be, I pity them. In a way, we're like them. We're stuck here, forever. We're not dead or alive."

Davin turned his back toward me with his shoulders slumped. I was tempted to reach out and comfort him, but I just couldn't get my hand to move.

After he wiped something off his face, he slowly twisted his body and continued with his questions, "How did you get through? Are you a secret gatekeeper? Or perhaps you're one of the Divine

Elders? No, that doesn't make sense. If I count you as one of them, then there would be thirteen. But there can only be twelve Divine Elders."

"What are you talking about? You're crazy." I scrubbed my face. He was driving me nuts.

Davin crossed his arms with a frown. "That wasn't nice. Say you're sorry."

His demand was humorous.

"No," I retorted.

"Fine. I'm leaving. If you don't follow me, you'll get lost."

"I doubt that. The castle is not easy to miss. Anyway, I'm not staying here. Now that I'm out of Halo City, I'll be on my way."

"And just what do you think you'll find down there? Are you going back to Aden?"

"No. I need to find my friend. She may need my help. I made a promise and I always—" I stopped. Why was I spilling my guts to a stranger?

"I'm telling you right now that you're not going to find anything you need down there. From what we've been told, the Fallen scattered, and those who were at the battle scene … well, let's just say there were no survivors."

His words hit me hard and guilt consumed me. Not being able to remember much of what had happened hurt, but to hear that Trinity died broke my heart. Though I didn't love her as she'd wished, she was my friend. She had been there for me when I needed her. I should have done things differently. I didn't know exactly what, but it was too late anyway.

17

I dropped to the dirt and covered my face with my hands, immersed in guilt and regret. I had no tears to shed. But if tears could have made those feelings go away, I would have wept freely. The pain was too much to bear.

Davin paced back and forth in front of me, rambling about something. He came toward me, but then backed away.

I stood up and started walking. I didn't know how to get out of Crossroads, but I figured I'd eventually find my way out.

"Hey." Davin followed on my heels. "Where do you think you're going?"

"I told you that I wasn't staying. Now leave me alone and go back to your group."

Davin somehow managed to stand in front of me, blocking my way. "My group? If you've forgotten, you're an Alkin too, unless you prefer to be a Fallen."

I kept my mouth closed and stared at him coldly.

He threw up his hands. "You think we want to be here? You were meant to be here. It's called fate. Instead of feeling sorry for yourself, why don't you use all that energy and do something good for a change? When you concentrate on being good, your heart will start to mend. Maybe not right away, but in time your heart will be filled with so much love that you won't even remember why the pain was there in the first place."

Davin's eyes held hope and desperation. I could tell how much he wanted to reach me, but I stood at the point of no return. No matter what he said or how much he begged, I was too stubborn to admit that I needed them.

"You'd be better off without me," I said and walked past him.

As I continued along the path, I tried hard not to look back, but curiosity got the best of me, and sure enough, he was gone. I didn't know why, but I felt empty, and in a strange way I missed him already. Until ... I turned to see him right in front of my face.

"Ha! You turned," he gloated. "That means you missed me." He smacked my back and wrapped his arm around my shoulders as if we were long lost buddies at a reunion.

I didn't miss him anymore. "Get off me." I shoved him off me.

Davin skidded backward. "You can say or do whatever to me, but I know you missed me. You missed me! You missed me! You missed me!" he sang repeatedly.

"Listen, I'm not going to be nice next time. You see this?" I showed him my fist. "It's going right to your face. Got it?"

Davin shut his mouth and backed away. I could tell from his expression that he was hurt. I closed my eyes for a second, but it was long enough for him to disappear.

I felt awful, but I trudged forward as his words repeated in my head: *When you concentrate on being good, the urge to be bad fades away. When you concentrate on being good, your heart will start to mend. Maybe not right away, but in time your heart will be filled with so much love that you won't even remember why the pain was there in the first place.*

I didn't know how long I'd been on the road, but I had to go back, at least to apologize. Or maybe that was just an excuse.

Chapter 4

After I found my way back to Halo City, I went looking for Davin. Since I wasn't familiar with the surroundings, I headed to the fountain. When I arrived, countless children were gathered around Margaret.

Margaret read them a story about a man named Daniel and a lion, and told of how Daniel's faith in God helped him through some frightening times. I thought, *if only I had faith like him, it would be so much easier for me to be here and to accept all that has happened.*

When the story ended, Margaret approached me with a smile. It was simply a warm gesture, but I froze. I wondered if she knew I'd left Halo City. She answered my question.

"So you've decided to stay after all. You've made the right decision. Sometimes you just need to stand back and look at the whole picture to figure things out. When our emotions are fired up, we can't think straight. Well, at least that is what I believe."

I couldn't look at her. She was being so nice and understanding. Margaret didn't lecture me or ask me a bunch of questions. She simply accepted me.

"Michael ..." She placed her hand on my shoulder. "... I know it's hard for you to understand why parts of your memory were taken, but you need to know that the Divine Elders do what is best for you. Sometimes the painful memories from the past can hinder your future. You must let go and move on. Learn from the past, but live for what's in front of you."

When I lifted my head, she smiled and left. I had just been told that the Divine Elders had taken my memories. That was the reason my memories had been fuzzy from the moment I first woke up in Halo City. Though I should have been furious, I took the news surprisingly well. I'd done many unforgiveable things with Aden. Perhaps it was a good thing I couldn't remember. For those reasons alone, I could find a purpose to move forward.

A small body wrapping around my legs brought me out of my thoughts.

"Michael," a little voice sang.

Peering down, I saw a sweet smile that melted my heart. She had long, curly golden hair, and her blue eyes reminded me of the sky. She looked to be about five years old.

"Hello there, little one." Bending down to her level, I gave her a sincere smile. "How do you know my name?"

"Don't you remember me?"

"My memories are hazy right now."

"What's hazy?" She tilted her head to the side.

"It means it's unclear. I can't remember much from my injury." It was only half the truth, but that was enough.

"Then I'll help you remember. You saved me from Aden. He tried to take the children too, but you hid me. You told me to stay there until help came. And-and you said you would come too and that you would be right behind me, but you never came. I was worried." She sniffed and tears glistened in her eyes.

Oh, not the tears. I embraced her and something strange tickled my heart, a sense of warmth and sadness. "I'm so sorry. I'm here now. I'm a bit late, but I'm here."

I released her and wiped her tears. She reminded me that I had done good deeds even while doing something evil. Perhaps there was something to salvage.

"So what's your name?" I asked.

"Alexa Rose."

"That's a beautiful name, Alexa Rose."

"Thank you. And you are very … handsome." She cupped her mouth and her cheeks turned pink.

I chuckled, and I might have blushed a little.

"Can you promise me that you'll be around and not disappear like the last time?" she asked.

I didn't like to make promises I couldn't keep. "I— ummm, I—" Davin's words kept replaying in my mind. I wished he would leave me alone. Not only did he invade my space by following me to the Crossroads, he was invading my mind too. But I had to try. There was nowhere for me to go, especially since Trinity was — I couldn't even say the word.

"I promise," I said. "We can even do a pinky promise." After I showed her, she giggled and skipped along to her friends.

"You'd better not break that little girl's heart. She's been through a lot," a voice said behind me.

It had to be Davin. I checked and yup, it was him all right. He tried to give me a stern look, but it came across as a goofy grin.

"I won't." I stood up.

"So, you decided to stay after all."

Recalling Margaret's words earlier, I asked, "Did you tell the Divine Elders I'd left?"

"Maybe I did and maybe I didn't. Why do you care?"

Just when I was beginning to think we could get along, he got on my nerves again. "Well, did you?"

His slight frown got bigger and his eyes became smaller. "Nooo," he dragged out the word. "And do you know why? Because they know everything." His angry expression became silly again. "And plus, it's a good thing you came back. You could walk forever and you'd never find your way out. You'd be walking in circles. Now that would've been hilarious." He chuckled.

I pressed my lips together. A small laugh fought its way up to the surface, but I wouldn't allow myself that joy. I didn't deserve it.

He held up his index finger. "And another reason it was a good thing you came back."

"Why?"

"You're an Alkin. Once you've crossed over to Halo City, you'll always depend on this light to retain your angelic powers. You can't remain on Earth for long periods of time. How long is too long? I have no idea since I haven't been down there since I was taken. It's a sure way of keeping us on track."

I tried to register what he'd said. I should have been extremely upset, but I wasn't. There was no way I could go back, not permanently, if what he said was true. And I believed him. He had no reason to lie to me.

Earth had nothing left for me anyway. I had no choice but to stay, and I guessed that was a good thing.

"Michael." Vivian appeared with Caleb alongside her. "We're so happy you've come out. Has Davin been showing you around?"

Davin said, "Yup. We're having a blast."

I wasn't sure if his tone was sarcastic or sincere. He was tricky that way.

"That's fantastic. You two are getting along," Caleb gave Davin a look I couldn't read.

"Yup, just hanging out with my new best buddy." Davin swung his arm around my shoulders, gripping me tightly, yet not in a pleasant way.

Wanting to give him the same loving feeling back, I flashed my wings open. Davin flew across the space, right into the fountain. Vivian, Caleb, and some children who had witnessed the event laughed like there was no tomorrow.

When Davin sprang out, I thought he would come at me, but instead he chuckled out loud. "Ha! I made you all laugh. I meant to do that."

Water dripping from Davin's clothes, he came over to where I stood. With a smirk, he said, "I owe you one, Michael. This is war."

Great! What did I get myself into now?

Chapter 5

I stood beside the Divine Elders and the officers and faced countless Alkins below the podium. As I wondered why we were there, Phillip took a step forward.

"I've gathered everyone so that you may officially meet our new member. He will be one of the officers. He is also a descendant of one of the Divine Elders. You might have already met him. I present to you, Michael."

The Alkins cheered and clapped. I waited for some other Michael to come forth, but no one came. Davin nudged me forward. Phillip meant me? Had I known I was going to be introduced like that, I would have locked myself in my room. Not wanting to disappoint the crowd, I raised my hand and gave a fake smile.

I frowned, but tried not to show it. Not only had I been appointed as an officer, but I was a descendant of one of the Divine Elders. *Great! Could this day get any better?*

After Phillip finished his speech, which I only half listened to—something about me training Alkins in

27

sword fighting—I went straight to my room. Looking up at the ceiling as I lay in bed, I thought about my options.

One, I could find a way to get out. But where would I go, especially since I couldn't stay on Earth for long? Or two, make the most of it. Like Davin had said before, the only way to mend a broken heart was by doing something good for others.

Being good with a sword, I could teach the Alkins. I could give them skills to be better fighters, so if and when another battle arose, we would be ready. It was the least I could do, but the thought of being descended from one of the Divine Elders boggled my mind. Although I knew that angels were not to acknowledge their descendants, an unexpected dagger twisted deeply in my heart.

Someone barged through my door. I should have known; it was the thorn in my side.

"What do you want, Davin? Don't you have any manners? Have you heard of knocking?"

"How am I supposed to answer all three questions at once? Hmmm, let me try. Sword fighting, yes, and yes." He chuckled. "I've brought you your sword."

That got my attention. Bolting out of bed, I stood there in disbelief, but I saw it with my own eyes. I didn't know why Davin was there or why he was willing to give me my sword, so I closed the gap between us and extended my hand.

"Here," he said and handed it to me.

After examining it thoroughly, I confirmed it was mine.

"Are you going to put that thing to good use?" he asked.

"What do you mean?" I knew what he meant, but I wanted to mess with him a little. I hadn't noticed it happening, but it was easier to joke with him. I relished his friendship, though I would never admit that to him.

"I saw the look on your face when Phillip mentioned that you would be training us to be better sword fighters. You looked like you were going to piss your pants."

I couldn't hold in the laughter. I chuckled out loud. I knew exactly what face I'd made.

I pointed my sword at him. "Maybe I will and maybe I won't. Maybe I'll help everyone *except* you."

The right upper corner of his mouth curved up and he squinted, like I was too bright for his vision. "Fine, but let me tell you this, I don't need your help. I'm the best there is."

"Really?" I challenged, twirling my sword. "That's probably because you haven't seen what I can do."

"Well, I owe you one."

"Owe you one," I repeated under my breath. That had a familiar sound.

My backside slammed against the floor. Too engrossed in getting back a part of my past, I'd let my guard down. Davin had used the same technique that I had used on him at Crossroads, and swung his legs around to knock me down.

Before I had the chance to retaliate, he ran out the door, leaving it open. His laughter rang through the hallway.

29

"Catch me if you can, chicken." Then chicken squawks replaced the laughter.

That little dimwit, I was going to teach him a few things. After I turned a few corners, I jogged into a larger room, where I spotted him.

"You're not fast enough," I said, pinning him against the wall. But to my surprise, I was the one not fast enough.

"You want to say hello first?" Davin smirked, gesturing behind me with a nod of his head.

I released him and turned to find countless Alkins standing at ease with swords in their hands. Though I had already made up my mind to train them, Davin hadn't known.

I didn't know if I should be thankful he cared or irritated he had tricked me. I would have to give him more credit in the future. Not only was he a thorn in my side, he gave me hope and a sense of belonging. Yeah, I had to admit to myself, I was actually starting to enjoy his friendship, just a little.

Davin expected me to walk out of the room or give him a piece of my mind, but I wanted to surprise him. So instead, I greeted everyone and began lesson one: the basics of handling a sword. Ironically, one of the skills Aden had taught me.

Davin didn't say a word, but he tried to hide a goofy grin as he headed toward the back. After several rounds of demonstration and having them spar with each other, I decided it was enough for the day, or for one session, since I had no sense of time anymore.

When everyone had dispersed, I headed toward my room. On the way I peeked into the rooms that had their doors open. They were all pretty much set up the same, but one caught my attention. Humbled by the sight of a female figure sitting in front of a large canvas popping with vivid colors, I stared wordlessly.

"Come in, Michael," Agnes said. Sitting on a stool with her back to me, she dabbed paint onto the oil painting of a garden in full bloom. "Do you paint?" Agnes asked. Her eyes were still glued to the canvas.

I leaned my shoulder against the doorframe. "No, I don't think I have, at least not that I can remember."

"You should try it. It can help clear your mind, give you a sense of tranquility, and even let you escape this crazy world we live in. And I'm not talking about Earth, I'm talking about here." She laughed. With her lips pursed, she layered a stroke of paint onto a pale pink flower petal. "So how was training?"

"You know?"

Agnes swiveled on the stool to face me. "We know everything, Michael. Well, almost everything. I think it's brave of you to take this challenge. That alone is brave enough. I can also perceive your heavy heart. You're struggling with the knowledge that you are a descendant of one of the Divine Elders. I wish I could tell you everything, but I promise you, when you are ready, it will all come together. "There will be more challenges ahead, but it's how you overcome them that builds character. Anyway, I hope I didn't bore you too much." She waved her paintbrush and pointed at the canvas.

"I'll have painting tools ready in your room," Agnes said. "You don't have to start right away. Just let inspiration guide you. It will come when the time is right."

"Thank you, Agnes." I left the room, but I wanted to say more. I wanted to thank her for her forgiveness and for not judging me, mostly for giving me a second chance I didn't deserve.

Chapter 6

Every day I trained the angel warriors. Caleb, Vivian, and even Davin helped and we enjoyed our times together. Sometimes Davin got on my nerves, but I knew he was trying to be jovial. It was more my fault than his. All four of us hung out a lot together, but somehow Davin and I had become especially close. Though I never told him, I was grateful for his friendship.

I was in a much better mindset than the first day I'd arrived in Halo City, but sometimes the guilt got the better of me. During the solemn times, I soared across the sky alone, but today, I parted the grass and passed through.

"What are you looking for?" Davin slapped my back.

I flinched. Turning to him with a scowl, I said, "None of your business. I didn't invite you here. Go away."

"So you're having a party without me?"

"Did I say I was having a party?"

"No, but you said invite. You only invite when you have a party. So where's the party?"

I took a deep breath. He was trying to annoy me on purpose. "I want to know why these beings come here. I wanted to speak to one."

"What? Are you crazy? You can't—I mean, you're not allowed. Don't you know the rules?"

"What rules?" I asked, checking for any wandering souls.

"You're not allowed to touch them or speak to them. You could—" He paused. "Actually, I don't know why. We were just told, so we listened."

Hearing only half of what he had said, I concentrated on a light that had appeared in the distance. After the glow faded, a little girl about Alexa Rose's age stepped forward.

"That never happened before." Davin seemed curious too, inching closer.

"What never happened?" I asked.

We moved closer to the grass, but remained hidden.

"The light. I've never seen one here before." Davin rubbed his temples, keeping his gaze on the little girl.

"You mean you've been doing this too?"

"Well, I wanted to speak to one, but I never did. 'Cause we're not supposed to." Davin's tone became stern. "I don't want to get in trouble."

Ignoring him, I continued to stare at her. This little girl had me under her spell. Something about her captivated me. I sensed a strange connection to her as I watched her searching, looking lost and confused.

Wanting to help her, I nudged forward, but something held me back.

"Are you crazy?" Davin shook me. "What part of 'I don't want to get in trouble' didn't you understand?"

"Davin." I bored my gaze into his. "Don't touch me and don't stop me. I want to talk to her."

Davin furrowed his brows. "Michael, you don't have a thing for little girls, do you?"

"What?" I snapped.

"You know, old men liking little girls. You're not a pervert, are you?"

"No! What gave you that idea? You're crazy."

We stopped arguing when the light blinded us and then it started to fade.

"Nooo," I whispered under my breath.

I had missed my chance. Davin was always in my way, always trying to keep me on the right path. Then, when I mulled over his intentions, I realized they were good and I calmed down. "Davin, next time, don't stop me."

"Or you'll what?" He shoved his face into mine.

"Never mind." Somehow, I knew she would come back. Then I said in my mind, *You're a pain.*

Davin looked at me strangely. "I'm not a pain. And how did you do that?"

"Do what?"

"You spoke to my mind. You had a conversation with my mind and you didn't even open your mouth."

"You're crazy. You're hearing things." I walked away.

"Do it again."

"No." I pushed through the grass.

"Chicken," he said, following me.

There he went with that chicken word. "Fine." And so I did, just to get him off my back. I said something in my mind.

"What? I'm not a fart face." Davin chuckled.

"I didn't say that." I stepped on the sea of clouds.

"Got ya!" He chuckled again, matching my steps. "Awww, I love you too." He tried to give me a hug.

"Get off me. Now who's the pervert? And I didn't say I love you."

Davin's eyes glowed with admiration, and his tone became softer. "You're truly one of the Divine Elders' descendants."

"Yeah, well, it's no big deal. So don't tell anyone."

"Why?"

I walked faster and glanced over my shoulder when Davin lagged behind. "Can't you do as I ask instead of asking me why every time?"

"Nope."

"I didn't think so," I expanded my wings, ready to take off. "I don't want others to view me differently." I wanted to blend in and not have everyone look at me the way Davin had.

"Others already look at you funny, so what's the difference? Okay. I won't. Oh, by the way, don't call me chicken. That's what you said to me in my mind. That's my line."

I chuckled and took flight. As usual, Davin followed me.

Time after time, I went to the same spot and waited for the little girl. Her visits were always fleeting, only to disappear as quickly as she'd come. Trying to guess when, or even if she would, proved impossible.

Alone on the dirt road, I was about to leave when light caught the corner of my eye. The light disappeared and the same girl materialized, only she wasn't little anymore.

Had it been that long since she last appeared? Her face had matured and her brown hair hung past her shoulder blades. I felt a connection with her, as if I already knew her.

Many wanderers passed by, as Davin had said, but something was different about her. No one else appeared with the light, and to top that off, she aged like a human.

"There you are."

I jumped. Too engrossed in watching the girl, I hadn't sensed Davin's arrival.

"Stop following me," I said. Surprisingly, my tone was gentle.

"Whoooa, that's not the same girl, is it? I mean, it looks like her, but older. How's that possible? Unless she's a real human."

Davin and I both held our breath when she came closer toward us. She tried to push through the grass, but she couldn't, then she started to fade. Davin and I finally snapped out of it and exchanged wary glances.

"Don't tell anyone," I said.

"Why?"

"Because I said so," I said sternly.

"That's not nice." He crossed his arms, frowning.

"Okay." I changed my tone softer. "Please don't say anything to anyone."

"Why?"

I counted to five in my head to calm my nerves. "Listen, I think she's different. I think it's best we let her be. She's here for a reason."

"Yeah, for your entertainment. I see the way you look at her."

My nostrils flared. "That's not the reason. Stop thinking perverted thoughts."

"You're not nice again." He lowered his head.

"You're not making this easy. Please trust me and do as I ask."

"Okay, since you asked nicely. And I do trust you."

His words tugged at my heart in a good way, and the irritation that had consumed me disappeared. Then we flew across the breathtaking clouds.

Chapter 7

The Alkins' sword fighting skills had improved. I was proud of what I had done, but I reminded myself it was my duty, the least I could do to make up for my past. And sure enough, Davin was right. My heart started to heal. The ton of bricks on my shoulders lightened.

As promised, Agnes left painting tools on my table, but I didn't lift a finger to try them out. I had no inspiration. No desire. So I left them there for days, weeks, or maybe months. I didn't know.

When I had free time, I read stories to Alexa Rose and her friends. They were a joy to be around. I felt their innocence, their pure souls that made my heart content and full. Children reminded me that good lived in the world.

I had just finished a training session and entered the garden to get to my room, when I saw Caleb and halted by the fountain.

"Hello, Michael. I enjoyed our lesson today."

"Thanks," I said.

Sometimes the thank-yous and appreciation from the Alkins left me flustered. My cheeks felt warm, and though the feeling was nice, I wasn't used to it.

I focused on water in the fountain. "Hey, Caleb, why does the water sparkle like that?"

"If you look carefully, there are tiny crystals. The Divine Elders' swords are made from these crystals. These special crystals darken if a Fallen is nearby."

That proved I wasn't a Fallen anymore. The crystals didn't darken at my presence. But the thought that they would change color intrigued me, and for some reason the little girl from Crossroads entered my mind.

Did she need protection? I'd heard of special beings with special souls. Could she be one of them?

"We're having a gathering in the meeting room," Caleb said. "Would you like to join us?"

"Will Davin be there?"

"Yes."

"I need to take care of something first. I'll see you there."

I felt bad lying to Caleb but I wanted to go to the dirt road. Something tugged at me and I had a feeling the girl would be there.

As I was about to leave, the crystals sparkled in the light. No one had said I couldn't take them. I scooped up a handful and snuck them into my room. I hid them underneath the covers before I left for Crossroads.

When I arrived, I went to the same spot and waited for her. I didn't know how long I had been there, but if I didn't leave soon, Davin would be looking for me.

Perhaps I had missed her, and she had come and gone.

When I rolled my shoulders and fanned out my wings, I spotted the light in my peripheral vision. My heart pounded out of my chest and tingles zapped through my stomach. My breath was short and a giddiness consumed me.

She looked more like a teenager—taller and her body filled out beautifully. What was I thinking? I had feelings for someone I had never met—not only that, the feelings were forbidden.

Before I started to lose my mind, I needed to leave. I flapped my wings, ready to take flight, but she came closer. Her sad expression forced me to stay. Why was she so sad? It pained me to see her that way. I wondered what she was going through.

When she started to push and shove the grass to enter, I wanted to reach out to her, and I almost did. It took every ounce of my will to restrain myself. Before I did something I would regret, I soared to the clouds.

As soon as I arrived back in Halo City, I went to the meeting room and joined the gathering. Alkins filled the room, mingling in groups. When I spotted Davin, I went toward him.

"Hey," I said to his group.

They greeted me with smiles.

"Where were you?" Davin asked.

"I was in my room."

Davin pulled me aside. "No, you weren't," he said matter-of-factly.

"Yes, I was."

"Then how come when I went to your room, you weren't there? I know you went back to Crossroads, didn't ya?"

It was difficult to lie to Davin when he gave that goofy grin, somewhere between joking and serious. I wanted to laugh every time I saw that expression, and I believed he knew it.

"Listen," he continued, "I asked Margaret about those souls that wander in that area. She said that sometimes humans wander there, but they pass over through their dreams. She said to let them be. If we allow them to cross over, their auras will be different when they go back and then there would be the possibility that the Fallen would think they are one of us. That means we would be putting them in danger. So just don't go back there anymore. If you don't see her, you'll forget about her. Got it?"

I gave him a curt nod. "Yeah, you're right."

Davin looked surprised and even a bit proud of himself that I'd given in.

"I need to stop by my room. I'll catch you later," I said.

When I got to my room, I took out the painting tools and started to paint. I'd never had lessons, but somehow, I knew what to do. I wanted to paint *her*.

The unnamed girl inspired me, motivated me, and sparked my desire. Though I tried to forget her, she had some sort of hold on me. But whatever the reason, I knew something great was about to happen. I couldn't even describe what that something great would be, but it was coming.

As the paintbrush stroked along the canvas, I lost myself in a world where only she and I existed. Peace and happiness held me, and I was no longer an angel. I was just Michael, and that felt good. But I agreed with Davin that I needed to forget her, for her own sake, so I made up my mind to visit her one last time, to say goodbye.

Saying goodbye wasn't as easy as I'd anticipated. I told myself it would be the last time, but I'd find myself back at Crossroads to see her smile, which became bigger when a butterfly danced around her. Her visits had become a lot less frequent during her teen years, and I wondered if she'd eventually stop coming. I didn't like that thought at all.

The light started to glow the way it always did when she came and left.

"Claudia, don't go," I whispered under my breath, then wondered how I knew her name. Since I'd come to Halo City, I'd discovered new talents. Was Claudia her name for sure? I would never know, but that would be her name to me.

I could see right through her as if the brilliant sun framed the outer lines of her body, blinding me. I took a deep breath and let out a heavy sigh, knowing she would disappear. Then she vanished, leaving me utterly empty.

"Michael!" Davin called out from a distance. "What are you doing?"

I ignored him as I continued to gaze into the empty space, trying to figure out what I was feeling.

"Michael," Davin called out again.

Knowing Davin would make his way to me, I broke away from my thoughts. "I'm coming!"

Walking away, I felt tangled emotions I had never experienced before.

Chapter 8

Back at Crossroads, my heart pounded out of my chest and my stomach quivered at the sight of the girl. I didn't understand the feeling, only that it happened around her, or when thoughts of her consumed my mind.

As I peered through the only thing between us — endless tall, thick grass — a feeling of ecstasy shot through me and I gasped. It was as if she had wrapped herself around my soul and held me spellbound. But would she finally find a way to cross over?

She wasn't smiling like the last time. Instead, her eyes lit up with determination. As she pushed and shoved to find a way to enter, a gust of wind swept through her long hair. It shimmered in the light, tousled in the gentle breeze, and brushed softly against her delicate face. Her striking simplicity took my breath away. I saw a flawless painting, and I couldn't believe she was there again.

A part of me wanted her to give up, but the other part of me hoped she would push through. She didn't know that I had watched her grow up, and she would never know I existed if I didn't make it happen. Who knew how much time would pass until her next visit?

As I continued to watch her struggle, I thought how easy it would be for me to reach out and touch her hands. It took every ounce of my willpower to hold back.

When it seemed as though all her energy had been spent, I couldn't hold back any longer. I parted the grass and walked out. Our eyes locked and I felt myself float above the ground. Time stood still as she continued to stare back at me.

What was she thinking? I had to know. Most likely she was in shock at finding someone coming out through the field. I had waited to speak to her for so long. I wanted to reach out and take her in my arms, but that wasn't something you did when you first met. She would think I was crazy.

I realized then I had put her in danger. *What have I done?* Furious at myself for being careless and putting my wants over her safety, I reacted quickly to fix the situation.

"Don't you ever give up?" I said.

She continued to stare at me.

"Ummm," she finally said.

I didn't know what to do. I had crossed the line, and I couldn't undo what I had done. I looked around for Davin. He was most likely spying on me and hiding somewhere nearby.

"What are you doing here? Do you want to be sent back like before?" I immediately regretted asking such a stupid question.

"First of all, who are you? And what are you doing in my dream?" she snapped.

I was amused by her spunkiness. She had no clue what I was. She didn't even know that what appeared to be her dream was real. I had to refocus and send her back quickly. Being rude to her might work.

"Your dream? You think this is a dream? Think again," I said in a condescending tone. The abruptness in my voice seemed to make her angry. Perhaps my plan wasn't working. She looked more upset, like she didn't want to leave. Maybe I needed to try harder. "Can't think fast enough? The answer is not on my face."

Her jaw fell open with a shocked expression. She looked even more furious. I was doing it all wrong. It wasn't working.

Her nostrils flared and she poked my chest. "I'm dreaming, and you're not real."

"I'm real. There is no doubt about that. And you may think you are dreaming, but you are actually at Crossroads, somewhere between Heaven and Earth or between life and death, whichever you prefer."

"That's not true!" She poked my chest again. "There is no such thing, and this is my dream … perhaps a nightmare after meeting you."

I gave her a cold stare. But now she thought I was her nightmare. What to do? Maybe if I told her that I was leaving, she'd leave too.

"I see. Perhaps I'll just disappear."

"No, please." She reached for me, but then dropped her hands to her side. "Wait. Don't go. I don't understand what's happening. Could you at least tell me how I got here?"

I arched my brows. "If you don't know, how am I supposed to know?"

"Well, I thought … I thought because you seem to live here?"

"Don't assume anything," I said sharply. The grass shuffled, giving away another presence. *Davin, I know you're there*, I said telepathically to him.

She's cute, Davin said in my mind. *Wait a minute! She's not supposed to be here. Can I meet her?*

Be quiet and go away. I've got this handled.

It sure doesn't look like it to me. Davin chuckled. *It looks like she got right under your skin. Michael, you're under her spell. I've never seen you like this before.*

I ignored Davin.

"Is there anyone else I can talk to that may give me some answers? Perhaps someone…*nicer*?"

Me, me, me! Davin thought excitedly. *I'm much nicer than Mr. Rude. He's in love, but doesn't want to admit it. Talk to me. I'll be the nicer guy.*

I shuddered, fuming. I wished I couldn't hear him.

"No. There is no one else here," I said.

"Really?" she fired back, looking skeptical. "You're telling me you're the only one who lives here? So you're absolutely alone?"

He's lying. Davin's mental voice sounded furious. *I'm here too.*

Go away. This is not your conversation.

Though she fumbled her words, she looked so adorable I had to contain myself from pulling her into my arms. But I had to get her out fast.

"I don't need to tell you anything, but if you must know, my answer is still the same."

She crossed her arms. "You're unbelievable!"

"I know I am," I said matter-of-factly.

"I didn't mean it in a good way!" she replied coldly.

Ohhh, she got you there. Davin chuckled. *Good one. I like her.*

Ouch! She'd burst my ego and Davin wasn't helping. "I did," I said with my chin held high.

She stared at me as if I had hurt her feelings and I felt bad. "You are just ... just ... just ..." She threw up her hands and paced back and forth.

Great job, Michael, Davin said. *Now she hates you.*

I wanted to reach out and apologize but before I could do anything, she parted her lips to speak.

Guilt ate at me and I softened my tone. "Do you have any idea why you are here?"

She halted in front of me and said, "No, I don't and I don't know how I got here. If you don't either, what do I do?"

I was close to losing it. I couldn't handle seeing her in pain. "Since I have no answers for you, perhaps you should go back." My tone was flat. "You shouldn't follow me, and you shouldn't be here. I don't care how you get back, but it's too dangerous here and humans are not allowed. You must go. Do you understand?"

I couldn't pretend anymore. It killed me to be rude to her. If only she knew what I was. If only she knew how long I'd waited to be in her presence.

49

I wanted to hold her close enough to feel her heartbeat and whisk her away to my world. She looked frightened, all the more reason to hold her and comfort her. But I couldn't. She hadn't moved, so I did the only thing I could do.

"You give me no choice. Davin, I know you're listening. Get her out now."

Ohh sure, Davin said in my mind. *First you want me gone and now you want me to do something for you. Fine!*

Stop talking. You're making this difficult. Just do it, please, before I change my mind.

A light glowed by her chest, and then it completely engulfed her. She became translucent and disappeared. I let out a deep, miserable sigh. She'd left with the impression I was rude.

If she remembered me at all, she would only have hatred toward me. Maybe it was better that way. We couldn't be together anyway. I would be chasing after a dream, a dream I wanted to be in forever.

"Let's go, Michael," Davin said. "If she ever comes back, I'll take over. You weren't nice at all. I mean, what guy in his right mind would say those words to a pretty gal standing in front of him? I guess you lost your mind when you saw her. You've really got it bad for her." He slapped me on the back and chuckled.

I let out a heavy sigh again, sensing an utter emptiness. "Don't tell anyone about her, okay?" I walked ahead, my legs dragging as if made of lead.

Davin walked beside me. "Don't worry, I won't. Besides, who would believe me? I make up all sorts of crazy stories all the time."

I snorted as we stepped on the clouds. "You sure do, my friend. But seriously, you talk about her and you won't be able to tell any crazy stories ever again."

Davin put a hand to his heart. "Why I'm hurt, Michael. Choosing a girl over me, your best friend?"

"She's pretty to look at and you're not."

"Speak for yourself."

"See you at the fountain," I said and took off before Davin could blink.

"Hey, wait for me. No fair, Mr. Rude."

I heard that, I told him telepathically.

Davin huffed an irritated sigh.

I heard that too.

Davin rolled his eyes. "Yeah, you would. And I meant for you to hear that!" Davin chuckled.

I saw that.

"How do you know?"

It's called ... I know you.

I arrived at the fountain first, then Davin appeared.

"What took you so long?" I teased.

Davin chuckled.

"What's so funny?" I said.

"I just realized it was the same girl. She grew up, and boy did she grow up. No wonder you looked at her strangely.

"What? You need to stop. Just keep your promise."

"What promise?"

"Did you forget already?" I ran my hand down my face in frustration. What had I done? I'd let her in. But I couldn't help myself. My emotions had overpowered my rational thoughts. She owned me. I couldn't go back there again for sure.

I narrowed my eyes at him. "Don't go back there, okay?"

"Okay," Davin mumbled under his breath. "But you let her in."

I gripped his arm, forcing him to look at me. "I'm serious, Davin." Davin looked at my hand, letting me know he didn't like how I held him. I loosened my grip. "Please. I let my emotions get the best of me. I shouldn't have let her in."

"Okay. I promise, but maybe I can talk to her and ask her why she keeps coming back. Maybe we can get some answers."

I shook my head. "I don't think it's a good idea. Just leave her alone."

"Okay," Davin said quickly and walked away.

I had a strange suspicion he planned to do as he pleased.

Chapter 9

I knew Davin was up to no good. When I didn't see him with Caleb or Vivian, and I couldn't find him anywhere, I headed for Crossroads. Sure enough, a glowing light appeared. Just in the nick of time.

"Davin! What have you done?"

Davin dropped his arms and moved around her, keeping his distance from me.

"Michael, I was only trying to—"

"Silence!" I snapped.

Davin and Claudia stiffened. I didn't mean to scare her. Inhaling a deep breath, I told myself to calm down. To control my anger, I rolled my fingers into tight fists.

"It doesn't matter," I said. "Now there is no turning back. Everyone will know."

Davin shrugged. "I was trying to console her and I got carried away. It's been ages since I've touched a human, and I couldn't help myself."

She looked at him strangely when he said the word *human*. Gaping between Davin and her, I noted how her cheeks turned slightly pink when I looked at her. She was shy, and I liked the feeling she kindled in me.

"You need to go back," I said softly, almost sorrowfully. I worried for her safety. When she didn't move, I turned to Davin and raised my voice so he would get the point, "Get her out, Davin. *Now!*"

"No. Why don't you do it?" he challenged.

"You know very well I don't have that kind of power. I'm not a gatekeeper like you. I can't send her back. I would do it myself if I could."

Davin paused, looking deep in thought. Then he looked at her. "Do you want to go back?"

I knew it! That scoundrel, he'd had this all planned. I shook my head and rolled my eyes as I waited for her to answer. Though I wanted what was best for her, I would rather her say she wanted to stay. When she shook her head, I hid my smile that crept up to the surface.

Seeming pleased with Claudia's answer, Davin said, "Michael, aren't you a bit curious as to how a human found a way to cross over from Crossroads? Besides, you asked for my help. I think we should take her to Phillip."

Liar. I did not ask for his help. Frowning, I responded carefully, "I don't understand it myself, but you know the risk we're putting her in. Do you realize what this means?"

"I know. I know," Davin nodded. His eyes flashed to the ground then to her. "Now the Fallen will be after her."

Telepathically I reminded him we needed to take her to Phillip. There was no time to waste once Davin had reminded me the Fallen would be after her when she returned home. Without warning her, Davin and I linked our arms through hers and soared.

"*Ahhh!* Oh my God!" She screamed at the top of her lungs as the wind whipped her hair. "You're flying! I'm flying! What's going on? How is this possible? Where are we going?"

"Are you human girls always this dramatic?" Davin snickered. "Sunday school sure didn't pay off for you. Don't you know your Ten Commandments? Thou shall not take the Lord's name in vain?"

She glanced between Davin and me as she spoke. "Are you serious? You're scolding me about the Ten Commandments? This isn't normal. What are you?"

Davin's lips twisted wickedly. "You don't listen very well, do you? I told you I'm an angel. You believe me now?"

For my sake, I turned to her with a cold stare. I didn't want to care for her. "You should have listened. I told you not to come back."

Chapter 10

"Welcome to Halo City, my human," Davin said to Claudia. He knelt down on one knee like an old-fashioned gentleman after we passed through the grand double doors.

Why hadn't I thought of that? Wait. I couldn't. I didn't want her to stay. I couldn't get attached to her. But when her face lit up, something warmed my chest and I hid my smile.

She gazed around, her eyes sparkling. "What are we doing here?" she whispered to Davin.

Thinking Davin might say something he shouldn't, I purposely avoided eye contact and said flatly, "You are here to speak to Phillip. He will know what to do. He knows you're here, thanks to Davin."

I didn't know if what I had said was true. I walked past her, accidently bumping into her shoulder—clumsy me. But touching her sent an electric jolt through my body. Not knowing how to react, I narrowed my eyes at her.

"Jerk," she mumbled quietly, but I heard it.

That stung.

"Well, I umm … well …" Davin shrugged and smiled innocently. "Don't worry about him. He's quite nice once you get to know him. He's somewhat of a grouch today, maybe because you're around."

"What?" She looked surprised and the sharp question came out louder than anything she'd said before.

Thanks, Davin. Now she'll hate me for sure.

As we waited for Phillip by the meeting table, I watched her from the corner of my eye. I was hyperaware of her presence, even the tiniest of her movements.

"Hello and welcome," Phillip said with an authoritative tone. "Please have a seat." He sat across from me and addressed Claudia. "I was wondering if you could tell me how you got here?"

She bristled and crossed her arms. "To tell you the truth, I really don't know, and everyone keeps asking me the same question." She flashed a frustrated glance at me and Davin, sitting on either side. "How come *you* don't know? You had to have seen me coming. Aren't angels all-knowing?"

I couldn't believe she'd blurted it out. She had courage. I liked that about her.

Phillip leaned back into his seat. "You see, I might have some answers for you, but I wanted to know if you knew anything first."

Her eyes widened. "You know how I got here?"

"Perhaps we can figure it out together." Phillip glanced at me and Davin. He telepathically let us know he was going to share information.

Inhaling deeply, he began.

"Humans only know a fraction of our history, although they spend years and years researching, trying to find concrete evidence of our existence on Earth. What I am about to tell you has never been disclosed to any human. Fair warning, if you decide to divulge this information to another human, they may think you have lost your mind. You understand what I'm trying to say, don't you?"

"Yes." She nodded.

"Very well, let's start at the beginning. I will make it short and simple."

Phillip explained the role of the Royal Council, Divine Elders, Earth angels, and Alkins, and how Halo City began.

Claudia seemed to take all the information thrown at her fairly well. As for me, I was so engulfed by her presence that I only heard half of what Phillip had said. Being near her was fascinating. Knowing she would be sent back to her home soon, I wanted to enjoy every minute with her.

"I know this is difficult to take in, but do you understand?" Phillip asked.

"What you are telling me is that there is a chain of command with angels?"

"Yes, at the top is the Royal Council, then the Divine Elders, followed by Earth angels. These angels have no wings. They blend in with the humans quite well, perhaps too well. Lastly, the forbidden children."

"What happened to these children?" she asked, looking concerned.

"They were sent here, this place called Crossroads, and you are standing in Halo City. Humans use the term Nephilim for these children, but we call them Alkins. Alkins are the alpha—the first of their kind, half angel, half human. They are the first generation to be born into human society."

When her eyes shifted to mine, I looked down. She knew he meant us, and I felt exposed, sort of ashamed, but I didn't know why. Perhaps it was her knowing I was a forbidden creation.

"Are you an Alkin?" she asked Phillip.

"No. I am one of the Divine Elders. When the Alkins were found, a few of us were reassigned to Halo City with them. It became our responsibility to guide and mentor the Alkins to be more like angels than humans. Margaret, Agnes, and I were chosen to become the Alkin mentors. The rest stayed behind to continue their assignments.

"How many Alkins exist here?" she asked.

"There are thousands of Alkins who reside here. I would like you to meet the officers who already know about you. The other Alkins are not aware of your presence, and I would like to keep it that way."

"Yes, of course," she said.

"I would like to introduce you to ..." The door opened on its own and they entered one by one as he motioned to them. "Vivian, Caleb, Ruth, Paul. And you've already met Michael and Davin."

Nobody said a word. There was an uncomfortable silence and the other officers looked stunned.

Phillip gave a casual wave. "You have to excuse their demeanor. It has been quite some time since they've seen a human. We're going to have to monitor you from here on. It's important we keep an eye on you, in case the Fallen find out about your involvement with us. You're an easy target since they can sense your presence now. Once you have entered our world, your aura will stand out from the rest of the humans on Earth. There's a possibility they may think you're an Alkin."

"Do you think it would be safer for her to stay here?" Davin asked.

Davin asked the question I wanted to ask but couldn't. Sometimes, he was helpful.

"She can't stay here. She is not an Alkin," Caleb said, looking upset.

"However, it would give us the opportunity to be educated about her world," Vivian said enthusiastically, next to Caleb. "Earth has advanced so much since we came here."

I shot Vivian a disapproving look.

Phillip folded his hands on the table. "I don't think that would be a good idea. You don't need Claudia in order to learn about her world. You can research on your own."

Claudia. Phillip would know her name, being one of the Divine Elders. Though I had called her Claudia in my mind for some time, I could be sure now. Her name rang beautifully in my ears. *Claudia* I repeated in my mind several times more.

"True," Vivian said. "But hearing it from Claudia would be much faster. And why wouldn't it be a good idea? Divine Commandments can be altered to fit the situation."

"She isn't one of us." Caleb sighed with irritation. "Need I remind you of the obvious again? What if the Fallen come here?"

Phillip was about to answer Caleb's question when Agnes and Margaret entered the room and everyone fell silent. Margaret stepped forward to speak.

"The Fallen can only enter our world if they take an Alkin who has inherited the soul of the Holy Spirit. Only Royal Council angels have the soul of the Holy Spirit. Isaiah was one of the Royal Council who fell in love with a human many lifetimes ago. His descendants now live with the Royal Council. I doubt any of them are left on Earth. The chances are slim to none that the One still exists. We do not make mistakes, so you need not worry. Hypothetically, if the One *does* exist, then it is out of our hands. And if the Fallen find the One, there will be war."

"Let the danger come. We're ready." Davin raised his fist in the air as if already victorious.

What was he thinking? Crazy Davin! Chaos erupted. Everybody started speaking their minds. A multitude of arguments filled the air.

Claudia rose out of her seat and raised a hand. "Can you please stop? I'll leave. Please don't fight. I'm so sorry." Her voice became softer and trailed off to nothing at the end.

She curled in her shoulders, looking intimidated. I didn't like how uncomfortable she looked.

Vivian went behind Claudia's chair. "Why not ask the human?"

"She has a name," I reminded. I hadn't meant to snap at Vivian, but Claudia looked nervous, and I wanted to make sure others didn't say anything to make it worse.

I guessed my temper had worked. Phillip said gently, "I'm sorry, but it's time for you to leave. We'll keep an eye on you as promised, to make sure you stay safe. However, this is an unprecedented incident. I can only hope my judgments are correct. Michael, I think it would be best that you be appointed as her guardian angel."

"What?!" Davin and I exclaimed simultaneously.

"Why?" Davin grumbled, shifting in his seat. "He doesn't even like her."

Thanks, Davin. Good going.

"*Like* has nothing to do with this, Davin," Phillip replied. "Michael is trained to be a guardian angel. And you are one of our gatekeepers. I need you here for now."

"I see your point." Davin inclined his head to the table, then looked up.

The frown on her face said she didn't want me to be the one looking after her. I turned to Phillip. "I don't think I'm ready to be a guardian angel."

"Nothing can prepare you for what you're about to do." Margaret placed a hand on my shoulder. "One can never be ready enough. Just listen to your heart and stick to the divine angel rules."

"You don't understand. I—" I bolted out of my seat, my chair scraping the floor.

Phillip cut in. "Nothing you say will change my mind. I've appointed you as Claudia's guardian angel, and that is final."

I stood there impassively. I wasn't ready. A glance at Davin didn't reassure me, and I looked at Claudia with defeat settling into my bones.

"Michael, wait." Alexa Rose came through the open door and passed by Caleb, Vivian, Ruth, and Paul.

This little one worried about me too much, but I knew why. I had told her that I would come back when I saved her from Aden, but it had taken me a long time to keep my promise.

"No need to worry, Alexa Rose, I'll be back soon. I need to take Claudia home, then I'll be right back," I said in a tone that would help her understand that I meant every word.

"Promise?" Her lips curled downward into a pout.

"I promise." I whispered something into her ear, making her giggle.

"Okay, I will," she responded cheerfully.

As Alexa Rose walked away, she acknowledged Claudia with a cute little smile.

Agnes placed a hand on Claudia's arm. "It's time to send you back. You're going to feel sleepy."

Claudia's eyes closed and her body began to sway.

Chapter 11

"Davin, send them back safely," Agnes said. "Michael, be on your guard."

I caught Claudia in my arms before she fell and wrapped her with my wings. At that moment, I knew I never wanted to let her go. Her scent and her warmth drove shivers through me. Standing in front of me was my dear friend, giving me funny looks.

"My human." Davin narrowed his eyes playfully as he took me to the dirt road.

I growled, but kept the volume down not to disturb Claudia. "Don't even start. She's not your plaything."

"I know." He shrugged. "It's just that she was so much fun to talk to, you know, like a friend."

"I understand," I said, gazing into her beautiful, peaceful face.

"Don't stay too long. Remember what I told you about how we can't stay on Earth? So don't run away or do something stupid."

I sighed and rolled my eyes. "I got it. You already told me that."

"I'm just making sure. You'll appreciate me one day."

"I doubt that," I mumbled, but I didn't really mean it. Before he could say another word, I soared across the clouds.

I moved from our world to hers. From out of the clouds, I took in the air that I'd missed. The wind brushed against my face, but I couldn't tell if it was warm or cold.

Agnes had told me the location of her house, and I entered her room through the walls. I laid her down gently on her bed and covered her with a blanket. Instead of leaving, I sat on the edge of the bed gazing around.

A desk was stationed by the window. Her closet to the left. She kept her room neat, clean, and simple.

My order was to take her home and go back, but I couldn't move. I wanted to watch her sleep. I gingerly brushed her cheek with my thumb, and just that innocent contact sent wonderful shivers through me, making me want to feel more of her.

In all my years, I couldn't remember anyone capturing my heart the way she had. I had suddenly awakened. I had to find a way to fight it.

I took my time running my fingers through her hair and whispering her name. Even saying her name filled my heart with raw bliss.

"I promise you with every breath I take, with every beat of my heart, I will protect you. I've done many bad things, but I was given a second chance for some reason, and I believe I'm supposed to be here for you. I have found my purpose for existing, and I will do everything in my power to be the best guardian angel. But it's going to be extremely difficult when I've already fallen for you."

Claudia stirred and I flinched.

I waited for her to settle back into deep, even breaths, and then I caressed her cheek. "I don't even know you, but I feel like I've known you all my life. I feel a connection that I can't understand. I'll be looking forward to seeing you again, but I hope it won't be because the Fallen have found you."

With much effort, I backed away and expanded my wings, ready to take flight. Speaking of the Fallen, I would make something for her with those special crystals to warn her of them. Recalling how butterflies made her smile, I decided to form the crystals into a butterfly pendant. A bracelet—no, easily breakable. A ring—too formal. A necklace—perfect.

Even with the certainty that I would be left with a broken heart, I didn't care. But I would take whatever part of her she was willing to give. Even knowing it was forbidden, I didn't care. The feeling was too good to be true, and I wasn't about to let her go.

"Claudia, can you hear me?" I whispered. "I'm not letting you go. I've surrendered to you. I'm completely yours. From this moment on, I belong to you."

I didn't know what had possessed me to say all those things, and I didn't know what possessed me to do what I did next. I leaned down and stole a kiss from her lips. It was a kiss to seal the deal, an imprint to say you are mine forever.

Was I ready to be a good guy, a hero? Phillip thought so. I guessed only time would tell. But I couldn't wait—I couldn't wait to get to know her. I already knew she had a kind heart. Angels could feel that. Forcing myself to leave, I already missed her, and like always when I left her, or when she left me, an utter emptiness consumed my heart.

Until next time, my love. I will wait.

Read how it all began for Michael. Book 1 (Crossroads) Based on author's dream.

Read sample of: (Fantasy Books by me)

*Crossroads (Michael and Claudia)
*Crown of Wings and Thorns (Michael is one of the main characters. This book is +18 and over.)
*ISAN
*Once Upon a Legend
*From Gods

Crown of Wings and Thorns
By Mary Ting
(Ask me about the story game app)

Chapter One
The Prison
Evangeline

"Wake *up*."

A deep, velvety voice filled me with warmth and love, but a mist covered him. I ached for a glimpse of his face.

"Two halves…" I struggled to open my eyes as my words drifted off in my dream.

"Wake up, Little Dove."

A tall striking-looking man with dark hair past his shoulders appeared in the haze—and then a blast of white light blinded me.

I gasped for air and shook out of my delirium. Groaning, I sat upright on hard-packed dirt layered with straw and blinked until the flickering torches hung by the metal bars and rocky walls of my prison came into focus.

Shit! I remembered my body swaying as if the floor had tilted, and then the world had turned dark.

How long had I been in this cell? Day or night? Impossible to tell with no windows.

My head pounded like a beating drum, and the stench of urine and feces turned my stomach. I gagged, holding in the urge to vomit, and pain surged up my chest. Something warm trickled down my hip. As I lowered my hand, the heavy weight of clanking shackles stopped me short.

Metallic gray cuffs made out of hematite crystal hung on my wrists, inhibiting my angel powers.

Damn these chains.

With a trembling hand, I dabbed at the wetness to gauge the depth of the gash under my rib cage. Thick, golden blood oozed through my skintight white uniform, between my fingers, and dripped onto the hay. The wound was deeper than I'd thought.

Even though the cut had begun to heal, the restraints around my wrists and ankles would slow my recovery time. I tuned my senses to listen for any clue about my whereabouts. Absolute silence.

Don't give up. Friends are coming. Unless they were captured too. But we wouldn't have all been captured, right?

A soft breeze stroked my face and caressed my long, gilded hair, but the brief comfort was shattered by the sound of a slap upon flesh. Soft whimpers came from the prisoners beyond the pitted brick walls.

"No, please." A man's desperate voice echoed. "I'll give you coins. Please don't touch me."

The captive was probably a hybrid offspring of a human and a lesser angel or low-class demon, or merely human. Either way, he would be assaulted and killed. Guilt pierced through my soul. There was nothing I could do to help him. Again, damn these hematite crystal cuffs.

Heavy footsteps thudded along the dark corridor. The feathers along my spine gathered in a tight bundle, ruffled involuntarily in warning of demons nearby. I pushed up to my feet, my knees wobbling as I retreated to the wall. It would protect my back, and no way would these soldiers see me on the ground like a groveling pig.

I widened my stance, holding the chains like a weapon, and slowly unfurled my wings through the back slits of my suit. It felt so good to loosen my muscles until pain radiated from the wound.

I swiped a finger on the dried splatters—crimson human blood and black demon blood—on my uniform. Similar stains dotted my alabaster and golden feathers. How many had I killed before they had captured me?

Five demon soldiers in human form stopped in front of my cell wearing smug grins. Hunters who had just cornered their prey. A baldheaded male with wholly dark eyes unlocked the metal door and jerked it open. I glared at him.

That one had dosed me with a sleeping potion before dragging me to prison. He was a fool for showing himself. I'd kill him first.

The other four soldiers positioned themselves around me with spears raised, but they kept their distance. They were no match for me even with the hematite cuffs. Their hearts raced and they smelled of fear. As they should.

"Ready to die, angel bitch?" The baldheaded guard scowled, the point of the spear so close I could touch it.

"Not by your hands, demon. I'll rip out your heart if you take another step." I wasn't in a position to taunt him, but I was never the docile type.

The baldheaded soldier growled and thrust his spear at my shoulder. I deflected it with a swipe of my raised cuffs, the sharp point of his spear brushed through my golden hair and lifted some dark strands in front of my face.

He roared as his fellow demons laughed mockingly. I didn't have full strength, but I could still use my wits, a weapon this fool lacked.

I pinned him with a warning stare. "Careful. Or better yet, come closer. Don't you want my blood? You'll be rich and you can have anything you desire."

His eyes grew wider and his thick tongue touched his lips. Then his features scrunched and he spat on the straw. "Don't get excited thinking you're going to trick me. We're draining Zander and your friends as we speak, so I don't need your blood. Soon, you'll all be dead."

Zander. Snow. Dawn. Tank. Otis. No! How? I had hoped I was the only one who had been captured.

I should have killed the underground demon leader named Gorgo when I had the chance. He'd asked to unite the Hierarchy of Angels and his kind to fight against King Asmodeus. But the archangels left Earth and sent out the Order of Angels, also known as OA, to finish their tasks. We were to remain among the humans until further notice—if we didn't die first.

As a Seraphim, I led my own team of mostly hybrid angels. Zander was the only other Seraphim on my team. Above me were hierarchy angels, also called superiors, and they gave us our assignments.

Our team agreed to the union with the underground demons and opened our home as a sign of good faith. They betrayed us. I'll never make that mistake again.

We had followed our escape route and thought we were clear, but the king's soldiers ambushed our makeshift home inside an abandoned barn. A wall collapsed during an explosion and separated me from my team. The others must have been bombarded when they exited the back of the structure. But all of them? *Impossible.*

"You're lying." Rage drove me as I swiped at them with wide, clumsy blows, the chains around my ankles slapping the dirt.

My boots weighed me down like they were encased in lead, and anchors bolted to the wall held me firmly as I strained against them. I didn't care if my skin burned and tore from the bindings. I didn't care if I broke an arm. The physical pain inside my rib cage was nothing to the agony in my soul. I *needed* to rip off their heads.

One of the demon guards slipped behind one of my wings, and I smacked him with a flap. Pain rippled up my spine and the gash tore even farther. But that soldier flew across the space and cracked his skull against the metal bars.

One asshole down.

"Shoot her. Now." The baldheaded demon pointed his spear at me.

The tallest soldier held a six-inch pipe to his lips and huffed. Something whizzed across the air and lodged in my neck. A tiny dart. I should have seen that coming. I would've if I had focused instead of acting from my temper and the emptiness where my heart once thrived.

If my team had been captured, all hope was lost. And if they were dead, I would join them in the afterlife. If there was such a thing for us.

"Time for your judgment, angel bitch." The baldheaded demon smirked. "I'm going to enjoy chopping your wings off."

The walls spun, and the soldiers doubled to ten. I drifted on a breeze, my soul a whisper in a meadow full of vibrant flowers. A peaceful place I created in my head. Hands tightened around me and the hematite crystal restraints clattered on the ground.

The king would execute me in a public display. There would be no trial. Angels had no rights in the human world.

Chapter (Once Upon A Legend) One

The Mausoleum

Merrick

ICY FINGERS OF GRIEF gripped my heart as I ran across the courtyard bricks with a stargazer lily in my hand. Crisp dawn air filled my lungs. Despite the biting wind, sweat dampened my forehead and heat surged under my skin. Chest heaving, I slowed onto the road that led to the royal family mausoleum, about a mile from the castle.

The circular tomb towered over the broad plain. Twelve massive pillars carved from the same gray stone held up the domed ceiling. Above the entrance a symbol, the Eternal Ring, had been etched. Six concentric rings, like ripples from a stone dropped in water, representing the six aspects of magic: soil, air, fire, water, light, and dark.

The sentinels painted on the outer wall held out their swords, protecting the royal dead. I stopped to read the adage from our ancestors etched along the archway of the iron door: *Death is only the beginning of our path to what is beyond. Enter with clarity. Enter with love. Enter to celebrate new life.*

I focused on the keyhole and curled my index finger, allowing a kernel of magic to flow through me with a warm, tingling sensation. The metal door creaked as it swung open. I took the first step down and swiped at cobwebs. The scrape of iron meeting stone echoed inside when the door locked behind me.

I stilled as a cold breeze stroked my face like a soft wave of ocean mist, and musty air tickled my nose. Swallowed up by walls built by long gone ancestors, I quickened my breath.

Breathe, Merrick. There are no ghosts in here. Don't be a coward.

Dust particles danced like butterflies within a shaft of light. The glass dome overhead not only let in the morning sun, but illuminated the painting of three stunning goddesses—Mothers Nimue, Viviane, and Myneve—on the glass, casting jewel-toned prisms over the caskets. Their hands interlocked on the hilt, the blade blazing a white fire. The Eternal Mothers' flowing dresses and their long silver hair glowed like moonstone against the light.

All former rulers of the Dumonian Empire and their descendants had been buried here. The most recent casket, my mother's, lay on a raised dais, circled by twelve steps. It had been months since illness had taken her life, but it seemed like only the day before.

I prepared my heart to be crushed again as I climbed the last steps.

"Your favorite, Mother." I swallowed hard and placed a pink stargazer lily on top of the glass casket over the spot where her hands crossed on her chest. I'd plucked one from the castle garden on my way every time I visited her.

Mother's face was almost alive. Her closed eyes were coated with teal, her cheeks with rose, and her lips ruby. Small, hammered-gold leaves intertwined with white baby's breath crowned her forehead and wove through her brunette hair.

She wore a long, alabaster dress, and she looked like a goddess in deep slumber. Regardless of how peaceful she appeared, my heart knotted with gut-wrenching pain.

Through Father's magic, Mother's body had been preserved. She would stay beautiful forever and so would the white rose petals scattered inside the casket.

"Mother, I'm here. You look like you're sleeping." As my words caught in my throat, I brushed my fingertip over the medallion Mother had given me before she passed away.

Mother almost knocked the water bowl by her bed when she fished something out under her pillow with a trembling hand. "My gift to you. You will need it one day."

Her fever never relented, even after all the medicine she had taken. The healer couldn't diagnose her disease or its cause. He'd only said that her illness could be a remnant of the Blood Plague that had killed so many infants the year I was born.

Mother uncurled her fingers, revealing a thin leather braid looped through a six-ringed silver pendant.

"An Eternal Ring?" I cradled the medallion with both hands. The polished metal, cold and smooth to touch, seemed ordinary, but Mother wouldn't have given it to me if it weren't special.

"This necklace was passed down within my family. I received it from my mother when she ..." Her weary voice stumbled on the final word. "Passed."

"Nonsense, Mother. You will get better. We just have to calm the fever." My weak voice faltered in its effort to give her hope as I tied the leather around my neck.

"No." Mother spoke with more energy than a sick woman should have. "Listen carefully." She pulled me closer until my ear rested on her fever-scorched lips. "The walls have eyes and ears. Be careful what you say. Trust no one, especially your father. Not even your brothers. One of your brothers will betray you. I've seen it in dreams. I have a gift of foretelling. No one knows, not even your father."

I jerked away, bristling at the seeds of distrust she planted. Father, Rodern, and Jediah, the only family I would have after Mother passed. If I couldn't trust my own family, who could I trust?

Mother was near death and delirious. She had been talking rubbish ever since she became ill, so I played along to give her peace.

"If your heart is worthy and pure, this pendant will help you in dark times," she said.

I wiped beaded sweat from her forehead with a

cloth and placed it back inside a water bowl. "How will it help me?"

"That will depend on you. It works differently for everyone."

I rubbed a thumb over the ridges of the six rings. In all the years we'd been taught magic, Mother had never once mentioned a pendant. It looked ordinary, though she claimed it wasn't. But how could I trust what she'd told me in her delirious state of mind?

What was so significant about it?

"Thank you, Mother. I'll treasure it forever." I shuddered a quiet breath, trying to remain strong, as her chest rose and fell with much effort. But her gentle smile said she was pleased.

Mother sensed my torment and rested her blazing fingers over my wrist. "It's okay, Son. It's what the goddesses wanted of me. Do not weep for me when I'm gone. I will be silently walking beside you, and I will always watch over you. I love you, Merrick. Even when I'm gone, I'll love you still."

Her whispered words slammed into my chest, crushing my lungs to leave me breathless. I dropped my head on the mattress and stripped away the man I'd become, down to the small boy for the last time, and let the tears fall.

I opened my eyes as my head rested against the cold, unforgiving glass of my mother's casket. Rolling back my shoulders, I shoved away the memory.

Trust no one, especially your father. One of your

brothers will betray you. I had become a prisoner of those words, always looking behind me.

After I gave Mother a reverent bow, I dashed down the stairs. Morning meal awaited, and Father would be expecting me.

I pushed the door open with a wave of my hand and sprinted out. Then I peered over my shoulder to ensure the door closed. As I admired the ruby-red glow stretching across the endless blue sky, I ran with Mother's love.

I knew her spirit watched over me. If she could talk, she would say … *Run, Merrick. Do not be late. Trust no one.*

ISAN-International Sensory Assassin Network

I ran to live.

Adrenaline pumped through my body as bullets whizzed by my ears and zigzagged past me, sparkling off the walls like fiery comets.

My feet pounded on the cracked tile floor as I charged down the hall of the decrepit building. With my team hot on my heels, I hurled over upturned office tables and broken chairs.

The air filled with a coppery tang, and I skidded to a stop when the hallway divided. Brooke let out an audible gasp, her eyes wide.

Justine grabbed her upper arm and flattened her palm against it. "I'm hit." She winced.

"How bad is it?" I asked.

Blood oozed between her fingers. Red specks splattered the dusty floor, and some landed on wadded up papers. Hopefully, her dark training shirt would catch most of it.

She snarled. "Never mind me. Do your job and get us out of here."

Justine liked to test my leadership. I wouldn't let her intimidate me. I knew when to bite back, and hard if necessary, a charming trait I'd learned from juvenile detention.

I released a sharp sigh. "Just make sure you don't leave a trail."

Calm. Steady the anger, Ava.

I glanced at the digital watch around my wrist. We had minutes left to reach the other side of the building before the clock ran out. *If* we didn't end up killing each other first.

"It's too quiet." Brooke's fingers travelled to her waistline in search of a gun. She'd forgotten Russ had declined to give us weapons.

"They went the other way, idiot." Justine rolled her eyes and wiped the bloodstained hand on her black training pants.

Brooke's hands curled into fists and her face hardened into a glare. "I can say whatever I want."

"You're not the only —"

"Quiet." I ground my teeth.

As I smeared sweat off my forehead, I listened for the clicking of guns and squeaks on the floor. Then the thunder of boots vibrated underneath me.

"This way." I sprinted down the hallway, tearing past a row of wooden doors scarred with chips of peeling paint and aged by time. When the corridor split again, I pressed my back to the wall as my hand scraped against the rough surface of the dilapidated wall.

As the soldiers' footsteps got louder, their precise location became harder to detect. The sound reverberated in a dizzying cacophony.

Justine tapped a foot, her gaze trained on my watch. "How much time do we have?"

"Six minutes," I said.

So little time. My heart pounded in my ears. I needed to make a decision. I stored a blueprint of the structure in my mind, and when HelixB77 serum had been injected in my system, the map appeared in front of me in the form of a hologram visible only to me.

I took deep breaths to keep from freaking out. The image flickered, then faded as fear took over. *Not now. Focus.*

Justine pointed at the air vent. "How about we go up there?"

"Are you nuts?" Brooke hiked an eyebrow. "What are we going to do, crawl our way to the exit door? Forget it."

I closed my eyes and tuned out their squabbling voices. *Breathe. Inhale courage. Exhale fear.* A few heartbeats later, I opened my eyes.

The intricate three-dimensional map of this structure hovered in front of me in a hologram. The building's layout, blind spots, all ten levels, the location of doors and elevators, and every exit point, all shimmered in cobalt blue.

There. The exit.

My pulse raced as I sprinted down the corridor, my feet slapping against the uneven cracked floor. I took the corner with a desperate spin, but halted abruptly. Six soldiers stood in a line, rifles pointed at our chests, their features tight, and eyes glinting with triumph.

"Raise your hands and surrender," the lead soldier said.

Each of us could take out two, no problem.

"Come and get me," I said, my voice smooth and deadly.

With a powerful kick, I aimed for the nearest soldier. He flew back, smashing his head against the wall with a sickening thud. He dropped his gun and I lunged for it as another soldier shoved it away with his boot, pointing his weapon at me.

Time seemed to slow as his finger tightened on the trigger. No sound but the deafening staccato of a machine gun firing. With a burst of strength from Helix serum coursing through my veins, I spun my body away from the incoming bullets, pushing off from one foot and planting the other on the wall behind me to flip backward out of harm's way.

The soldier I had originally kicked rose on his feet, stumbling. Before he could react, I rushed forward and punched him hard in the middle of his chest. He slid down the slippery floor, clearing the plastic water bottles and debris, and crashing into the pile of his unconscious companions that my team had knocked out.

"Which way, Ava?" Brooke's tone was laced with panic.

Footsteps thumped. More soldiers were on their way. I picked up a gun and my team did the same.

"The last one." I took quick, long strides and stopped at a door bearing a sign for the stairs.

I grabbed the knob with my clammy, trembling hand, hoping against hope it would open, but it refused to budge. Yanking didn't help, so I kicked the door in desperation.

Pain shot through my leg, but only for a second. It would have been worse if it hadn't been for Helix coursing through me.

What next?

"Move out of my way." Justine's eyes flashed with anger and her jaw clenched as she reared her leg back and unleashed a powerful kick. The door flew off its hinges and careened into the wall, splintering the frame in an explosion of wood, metal, and plaster.

I bolted down the steps, my team and the ping of dampened gunfire behind me.

Faster. Go faster.

Power and exhilaration surged in my muscles. I pivoted with my gun ready, but when there were no soldiers, I continued the descent and the footfalls pursuing me disappeared.

Twenty feet from the exit … eighteen … fifteen … so close … I could almost taste sweet victory, my heart leaping for joy. Then …

My watch beeped.

Damnit.

A deep rumble filled the air. The earth shook with a blast of deafening explosion, throwing us off our feet. Brooke and I slammed into the wall together and Justine barked a curse behind me.

Flames engulfed the stairs, blinding our exit. The smoke burned my eyes and tightened my throat. Another boom then a blast roared and I was tossed in the air again.

The structure groaned and shrieked as the walls crumbled around us.

I died.

Again.

Prologue
Michael
(Crossroads)
Book based on author's dream

There was something different about her.

Michael didn't know how long it had been since her last visit, but she had blossomed beautifully. All grown-up and perfect in every way.

The girl's eyes, radiant like the sun, drew his. Her long, brown hair shimmered in the sunlight, tousled by the gentle breeze, and brushed against her delicate heart-shaped face. Like a flawless painting, she was striking in her simplicity, and she took his breath away.

He had always watched her from a distance, a guardian protecting her so she wouldn't be found as a child. And like the past times, she looked lost, as if visiting for the first time.

She was unaware of his presence, and there wasn't a glimmer of a chance she knew he stood just beyond her reach. An endless field of tall, thick grass separated them, but would she ever be able to cross over?

It was nearly impossible.

Michael watched as she pushed and shoved, trying to pass through. But the elders had created one way in, and she would never know.

He reached out his hand to help her and stopped. It took every ounce of his will to refrain from letting her in. His fists tightened as he fought against what he wanted most.

The girl looked straight at him, her eyes sparkling like the luminous stars. Michael inhaled the moment as if she really *did* see him, for he knew her gaze focused elsewhere instead.

He imagined her sweet breath on his lips and gasped at his physical attraction toward her, wondering why he felt this way. The heat infusing his body wasn't anything he had felt or remembered, in whatever was left of his memory.

Michael was trained not to have these human emotions, and yet it confounded him how she appeared to have taken him over. He didn't mind at all. He liked the way she made him feel.

A butterfly landed on the tip of her finger, and she brightened with a heartwarming smile. The joy in her smile sent desire to every part of him. This human being held him spellbound.

If only Michael could breathe in her scent, embrace her in his arms, and feel her warmth just once, even if he could have nothing else of her. In the end, he knew it was hopeless.

Gradually, she started to become translucent, as if he had dreamt her. As always, she only stayed long enough for him to want her even more.

When would he see her again? With those thoughts, he desperately tried to memorize every detail of her before she vanished.

"Claudia, don't go," Michael whispered as he gazed upon a brilliant sun framing the outer lines of her body.

He let out a heavy sigh when she vanished, leaving him utterly empty.

"Michael!" a male voice called from a distance. "What are you doing?"

He ignored his friend as he stared into the empty space, trying to settle his racing pulse.

"Michael!"

"I'm coming." Annoyed by the interruption, he expanded his massive wings and soared across the clouds with tangled emotions he had never felt before.

Chapter 1 (Crossroads)
Claudia

A Year Later...

Swallowed up by darkness, my body levitated off my bed, floating higher and higher.

Is this a dream?

Then my feet touched the naked road and fine, smooth pebbles ground together under my step. The sun hung high in the cloudless sky, yet I felt no scorching heat from it. Nothing was familiar.

Where am I? Why am I here?

A field of sweeping green grass standing at least twelve feet high appeared out of thin air to my right. I had to bend my head way back to see the tips of the blades. Though I could only see the grass in front of me, it gave a sense of vastness. Like I could walk into the grass forest and walk for days without coming out the other side. When I lowered my head, I saw a woman walking in the distance.

Her presence grabbed me like a magnet, and I couldn't resist her pull. I sensed she was the sole reason why I was here, so I ran toward her.

She was a vision of pure splendor. Her flowing white dress reminded me of a Greek goddess. She wore her dark, silky brown hair tied up in a ponytail, not a single strand stood out of place.

I realized I hadn't seen her face, though I assumed she was beautiful. Something about her seemed … different. She began to pick up speed as if she sensed me closing in.

I pushed my muscles, ran faster, but no matter how fast I ran, I couldn't catch up to her. My legs weighed me down as if a ton of concrete had cemented them to the ground. Every ounce of energy I had couldn't help me catch this divine beauty.

Nearly crying with frustration, I watched her turn right and disappear into the field. I kept my eyes rooted to the spot where I thought she had entered, and when I reached the same place, I separated the thick grass and stepped in.

My breath left me in a gasp. A sea of clouds lay beneath me—fluffy, foamy whipped cream—like Heaven's clouds. Or magical clouds from a movie, the kind you could walk on without fear of falling through.

How beautiful this place was, but was this life for me now? Was I dead?

She appeared again, closer, but I still couldn't see her face.

She spoke politely yet with a sense of urgency. "Claudia, you need to leave. It's not your turn."

Shock slammed into me. The power of her words stopped me cold, and the trepidation in her voice jump-started my heart back to life with a lurch.

How did she know my name?

The fear piercing every bone in my body subsided, her words faded to insignificance as I stared at the fascinating vision standing before me.

Light shone around her, shaped like a halo and backed by translucent wings, which captivated me. The inner depths of her soul radiated from her in waves of goodness and light, pulling me closer.

Her face remained indistinct, blurred and obscured by the light shining from behind her. I desperately wanted to know what she looked like, so I stood there, ignoring her order, hoping maybe the light would fade. But instead, the light widened and intensified until it hurt, and I covered my watering eyes with both of my hands.

"Please stop," I pleaded.

She spoke again, but this time her voice turned unforgiving and commanding. "If you know what's best for you, you will leave now before it's too late."

Before I could say another word, a male voice shouted, "No, Margaret!"

I fell at the speed of light. Darkness engulfed me. My stomach leaped to my chest like I'd just gone over the steepest hill of a roller coaster. My body never seemed to catch up with the ride. I jerked to a split-second stop and then became still.

I had landed on something soft and familiar—my own bed. I peeled my eyes open one at a time. I tried to recall my dream before it faded, to analyze every detail I'd seen, for that was one dream I wanted to remember. One thing for sure, I would never forget the name Margaret, or the desperation in that guy's voice.

My heart jumped twenty feet into the air, jolted by the sound of my cell phone.

"What the—"

I placed my hand on my chest to calm myself and let the phone ring several more times. Of all the times to forget to put it on silent mode. I reached over to my nightstand and slapped my hand on the device.

"Hello?" I could have checked who was calling, but I was too irritated to bother with it.

This better be important.

"Claudia? Is that you?" Patty's voice rose to a high, elevated note, so loud I moved the phone away from my ear.

Instantly the irritation disappeared, but I couldn't make sense of what she'd said. After all, *she* had called *me*. Who else would I be?

Before I could say a word, she added, "I'm so glad it's not you. I'm sorry I called so early, but I had to be sure."

"What are you talking about?"

"You scared the life out of me."

I scared her? "What did I—"

Patty cut in. "I thought it was you at first. I don't know what I would do without you."

She thought I'd died? Had something happened to me? Was this weird phone call somehow connected to the bizarre dream I'd had?

"What happened?" I held my breath, worried what her answer might be.

"What? Seriously, you don't know?"

"Know what?" I sat up.

"Ohhh," she murmured. "You didn't hear?"

"What *happened*? I still don't know what you're talking about," I pressed.

Patty sighed. "Claudia Emerson died last night. You know, your friend who has the same name as you. You can understand my confusion when I found out, right?"

"What?" Blood ran cold through my veins. I didn't want to believe it. "Are you sure? Are you sure you got the right Claudia? I mean, I saw her last week. How could ... I mean ... I just saw her. What happened?"

Patty provided me with all the details of the incident.

Claudia had just been voted homecoming queen, and her date was the homecoming king. After the homecoming dance, they drove through an intersection on their way home when a drunk driver ran a red light and collided with their car. Claudia crashed headfirst through the front window.

I sat immobile, unable to move or speak as I tried to comprehend what Patty had told me. It didn't make any sense. It couldn't have happened. Claudia was not dead; surely it was a mistake.

"Claudia, are you there?"

"I... I... What?" I tried to come to terms with the gruesome story.

Patty continued, "I heard she wasn't wearing her seat belt because she didn't want to wrinkle her gorgeous dress. I wonder if she would still be alive had she put on her seat belt."

"I don't know. Did her date survive?"

"Yes. Do you know him?"

"No. I was just wondering." I sucked in a breath as I played the images of what Claudia's accident would have looked like.

"I won't be at church today. I'm scheduled to work all day. I can try to get out of work earlier if you need me."

"No. Don't worry, Patty. I'll be fine. Really, I'm fine." I tried to convince myself, too.

"Okay, but I'll come by after work. You may think you're fine, but I think you're in shock. I'll text you to let you know when I'm on my way."

"Sure, see you then," I said wearily.

Patty had started attending our church our freshman year. Her natural charisma drew people to her, and the way she genuinely cared made her friends with everyone. I couldn't recall how it happened, but we immediately became best friends.

Patty had delicate facial features and a sweet, pleasant voice when she wasn't screaming into the phone first thing in the morning. Her tall, slender body would make any girl envious. She was the kind of friend who would be there for me through thick and thin.

After we hung up, I thought about the "what-ifs." Like what if Claudia had worn her seat belt, if her date had paid more attention. If I had been the Claudia Emerson to die that night. I sat there, trying to make sense of what had happened to Claudia.

Like Patty said, I was in shock. You hear about things like that happening to other people, but never to someone you know. A quiet knock at my bedroom door took me out of my thoughts.

"Are you all right, Claudia?" My mother's voice reverberated through the wood. "I got a lot of phone calls wondering if you were in an accident last night."

"I'm fine, Mom, I'll be right out."

There must be a great deal of confusion over the death of Claudia Emerson, homecoming queen and now a drunk-driving victim.

What were the odds of having a good friend who had the same first and last name? It was strange at first, but I had gotten used to it since we had been friends and schoolmates since third grade.

After another quiet tap on the door, Mom spoke again, "We need to pick up Gamma, and we should get to church a bit earlier."

I opened the door. As I nodded to respond, the classic beauty of her face struck me. I guess I had never realized it before, but she didn't look like she was in her late forties. In fact, she could probably have passed for my older sister.

Mom's skin was as smooth as velvet, and there was not a wrinkle on her face. Her ebony hair reached just above her shoulders.

At times, I wondered what I would look like if I'd inherited her emerald-green eyes. But instead, I'd gotten my father's brown eyes.

I didn't know if I looked more like my dad than Mom, and I never would. We didn't have a picture of him. My parents had eloped, and shortly after, she got pregnant. Then my dad passed away in a freak car accident before I was born.

I hardly asked about him anymore since I knew it dredged up painful memories. My mother had it hard enough being a single mom, especially one working long hours as a nurse. Through it all, she never complained.

Fortunately for us, we had Gamma, my grandmother's best friend and also my godmother. I was just a toddler when my grandmother passed away, and Gamma filled the void by visiting frequently.

Gamma never married, so we became her family. She helped Mom and took care of me, especially when Mom had to work late shifts.

Gamma and I sat in the back while Mom drove us to church. We hardly spoke a word, but she held my hand the whole ride there as her way of comforting me.

The short ride seemed twice as long as the anticipation of getting to the church settled in my stomach. Still numb from Claudia's death, I walked toward my friends.

We hugged to say hello, but this morning it was a different kind of hug. They swarmed me with I'm-glad-to-see-you-alive hugs.

One by one, they got the physical confirmation they needed that I was alive. Then we stood there in dead silence. I guess no one knew what to say or how to react around me because Claudia and I had been so close.

Claudia had missed a lot of church, and we were starting to be more like acquaintances than friends. We had been best friends throughout junior high school, but our friendship drifted apart when we attended different high schools. It didn't matter though. The fact we shared the same name bonded us forever.

As if having the exact same first and last name wasn't odd enough, we also had the same hair color and were even the same height. Unlike me, however, she knew everything about boys and fashion, was more outgoing, and hadn't been sheltered growing up.

My thoughts drifted back to the last time I saw her. Why didn't I go up to her and give her a hug? The more I thought about it, the more pain bloomed in the pit of my stomach. Had I known I'd never get another chance, I surely would have held on tight.

A set of strong arms wrapped around my waist from the back. It was John, dressed in his usual T-shirt and jeans.

I looked up at him and noticed his hair looked two-toned under the sun—brown with lighter highlights. He gave me a half smile, and his body language showed uncertainty, as if he wasn't sure whether his closeness was appropriate at that time.

"Hey, Claudia. Are you okay?"

"I think so. I'm not sure. I don't know how I feel right now. It's like a dream. Did it really happen?"

"Yeah." John tucked his hands into his pockets and nervously changed the subject. "So where are we going for lunch?"

"I don't feel like going today." I glanced at the gray clouds overhead.

"Sure, I understand." He sounded disappointed.

The uncomfortable silence was unusual because John and I could talk about anything. None of us knew what to say as we stood next to each other. I wondered how long we would stand there when Marie broke the silence.

"Come on, we're gonna be late for Mass," she said.

I trailed in last. Overwhelmed with guilt, I stared at the cross and hardly paid attention during Mass. In fact, I couldn't even recall if I placed an envelope into the donation basket.

One thought replayed repeatedly in my mind: I would never see Claudia again.

I vaguely heard Father Roy speaking about the tragedy of Claudia's death, but I dwelled on the last hug I hadn't given or received, and the fact I shed no tears.

Didn't people cry when someone they cared about passed away? I tended to hide my feelings, but not feeling *anything* was next level. Perhaps the numbness would carry over and get me through the funeral.

From Gods

SKYLAR WAS ONLY eight years old, but she remembered it clearly as if it happened yesterday, when her whole world had been taken from her.

"Mommy, where's Daddy?" Skylar asked as they cuddled in bed.

"I'm going to tell you something and I want you to be brave." Her mom's voice cracked as she laced her fingers through Skylar's hair.

"Did something happen to Daddy?" Her heart pounded faster.

"He had to go away."

Skylar knew what her mom meant, but she needed to be sure. Had to go away meant he would come

97

back home soon. But an ache in the pit of her stomach told her something was wrong.

She jumped out of bed and looked out the window, recalling how her dad had told her she was beautiful like the sky. The golden moon and the illuminating stars calmed her nerves for a bit, but it did nothing to help her racing pulse.

"Is he... dead?" Skylar's fists clenched tight as she prepared for the news.

"No, honey. He has things to take care of."

Though she understood those words, she refused to believe them.

"Daddy is supposed to tuck me into bed and read me bedtime stories." Skylar sat next to her mom and hugged her arms to her chest, trying not to break apart. Because parents softened the bad news by coating it with a lie. And she knew her mom was lying.

"Sky." Her mom grabbed her hand.

She yanked her hand away. "Don't call me that. It reminds me of Daddy." Tears welled in her eyes. "Why can't he come home? Doesn't he love us anymore?"

As her lips trembled, tears poured down her face. Mom's words had shattered her heart into a thousand pieces. She had never felt pain like this before.

"Of course he loves you." Mom stroked her hair, tears glistening in her eyes.

The sobbing became uncontrollable and Skylar gasped for air. Her throat dried and her eyes stung, but she didn't care.

Mom wrapped her arms around her, trying to give

her comfort, but nothing eased the pain. Skylar wanted her dad to be home. She wanted the security and the daily routine. She wanted everything to be how it was.

From that day on, no one called her Sky, and her dad was dead to her.

SKYLAR CHECKED THE lanes for a police car. Driving down the highway at night made it difficult to spot one, but she didn't want to get caught texting. She wanted to let her cousin know she was almost there. Skylar and her cousin were best friends, and every summer she visited her.

Skylar
Can't wait to C
U.

A high-pitched sound rent the air. But when she heard the chirp of the siren signaling to get off the freeway, she looked in the rearview mirror and saw the reds and blues flashing and twirling.

Her pulsed raced. *How in the world? I was so careful. Damn it.*

She exited the freeway and drove into the first place that looked safe. A gas station. The only person pumping gas replaced the nozzle and drove off, leaving her alone in the lot with the cop. She wished she could follow the other car and drive away, but instead she parked away from the gas pumps.

No other stores bordered the station. In fact, it was pretty much a stand-alone building in complete darkness. Anything could be lurking. *What did I expect? I'm in East Nowhere, USA.*

Inside the station's mini-mart, the lights glowed, but there was nobody there besides the cashier. At least that made her feel safe—somewhat.

Skylar waited anxiously, biting her lip and thinking of ways to convince the cop not to give her a ticket. Tapping her foot and picking at her nails, she imagined her situation was like waiting for a courtroom verdict.

Being around cops intimidated her enough, but being pulled over by one was even worse. People got tickets all the time, but this being Skylar's first made it difficult to bear. How would she explain this to her mom?

As she waited for the officer, she wondered what she had done to be pulled over. It was almost impossible for him to know she had been texting. Her mind reeled with unpleasant thoughts.

What if he was a bad cop? What if he planted drugs in her car and made it seem like they were hers? More what-ifs circulated through her head—watching the news and bad movies had definitely affected her mindset.

Tap! Tap! Tap!

Skylar jumped, startled by the sound. "Sorry, officer."

She rolled down the window and then shut off the

engine. The flashlight shone brightly, hindering her view, but she got a breath of the hot, sticky air clinging to her skin. Even at night the weather was intolerable.

Hoping not to offend him or her, she shifted and got a clear view of his gorgeous, young face. With instant combustion, her heart fluttered a mile a minute and her stomach churned nervously.

Her face grew hot as she flushed, either from the sight of him or the searing weather—perhaps the combination of both. Whatever it was, his personal gravity pulled her in. She was wrapped in his invisible force and she was almost sure he looked back at her with the same intensity. *Breathe… breathe… exhale.*

She had heard of love at first sight, but this was more like lust at first sight. *What is wrong with me? Stop staring.* Sheepishly, she unglued her eyes from his beautiful greenish-blue ones. She couldn't tell exactly what color they were.

A pearl drop of sweat trickle down from his hairline. She didn't want to stare into his eyes again for fear she may get lost in them. So she focused on his uniform. It fit perfectly to the curves of his muscular frame.

His clean-shaven face brought out his cheekbones and every part of him looked flawless, from his hair to his broad shoulders, and all the way down as far as she could see. She had seen good-looking cops, mostly on TV, but for goodness' sake…

"Can I see your driver's license?" he said flatly.

Even the tone of his voice made her heart race. *Do you have a girlfriend?*

101

"Your driver's license?" he asked again.

Pause.

"Your license?"

"Oh, I'm sorry. This is my first time being pulled over. Did I do something wrong?" She focused on his name tag—Officer Doug.

"I need to see your driver's license." He sounded annoyed and I understood. He had asked me a few times already.

She reached into her purse and pulled it out from her wallet. "Here. It's really not a good picture."

The officer's lips formed a thin line. "We don't judge." He winked.

Skylar's cheeks flushed again and she wondered if he noticed.

"Skylar Rome?"

"Yes, that's me."

After staring for some time, he handed it back to her. "You're new to this town, aren't you?"

"Yes. No. Well, yes. I mean—" *I can't even talk.*

"Can't make up your mind?" The officer chuckled, obviously amused by her nervousness.

Skylar snorted. "I visit my cousin every summer. I was on my way there. Did I do something wrong, officer?"

He didn't answer, even though she'd asked twice. He seemed flustered, looking intently into the empty darkness as if he could see something there.

"Ms. Rome, can you open your trunk?"

"Oh, sure. I only have my bags in there." She reached under and popped the trunk from the inside. "Should I come out?"

"No. Stay there and don't move."

His stern tone startled her, but she didn't think much of it. After a few seconds, he came back. "Skylar."

"Yes?" She looked into his eyes and blinked, mystified. She could've sworn his irises had pulsated and turned silver.

"Don't text while you're driving. It's against the law if you didn't know."

"Sure." She smiled. "Thank you."

With a nod, he turned away and headed back to his car.

Skylar checked in her rearview mirror, but he had already gone. *That really happened, right?*

She took out her phone and read a text from her cousin.

Kayla
Can't wait.

Skylar
I got pulled
over by a
gorgeous cop.
He let me go.
Explain when I
get there.

Ecstatic that she hadn't been given a ticket, she put her foot on the gas and drove back onto the freeway.

⚡

KAYLA LIVED IN a two-story house. All the houses on the block were cookie-cutter homes, built practically touching each other. With hardly any streetlights it was difficult to spot Kayla's, so Skylar searched for not just her address, but also the white mailbox that glowed in the dark.

Skylar rang the doorbell when she arrived. Kayla swung the front door open and pulled her cousin in for a tight squeeze.

"I'm so glad you're here."

Kayla wore a gray tank top and cotton shorts. Her brunette hair brushed Skylar's face and she noticed it was longer than it had been on the last visit, now passing her shoulder blades.

"You grew your hair?" Skylar said, pulling back. "I love it."

Kayla flipped her hair in exaggeration. "Yours got longer too. Enough about our hair. So, what happened? A hot-looking guy pulled you over?" Her eyes beamed with curiosity.

"Hottest guy ever."

"Did he give you a ticket?"

Skylar swiped her hand across her forehead. "Nope. Thank God or Mom would've killed me."

"You got lucky. He probably thought you were cute and let you go."

How cool it would have been if those thoughts had run through his mind. But what did it matter anyway? What were the chances of seeing him again? Slim to none, she figured.

"So did you ask him to cuff you?" Kayla snorted.

Skylar shook her head, thinking how silly she'd acted. "I was too busy trying to get my mouth to work. I stared at him like an idiot."

"Let's talk in your room." She eyed the luggage on the floor. "Just two bags?"

"I'm only staying for three weeks, not a year. So where's your mom?"

"She's still at work. We keep the diner open until midnight during the summer." Kayla smirked. "So, did you get his name?"

Skylar gave a playful glare and rushed upstairs with her bags, Kayla at her heels.

After Skylar had settled into the guest room, the girls sat on the bed and discussed their summer plans.

VESUVIAN BOOKS (Publisher)
ISAN - International Sensory Assassin Network
Helix (Book 2 of ISAN)
GENES (Book 3 of ISAN)
CODE (Book 4 of ISAN)
AVA (Book 5 of ISAN)

Jaclyn and the Beanstalk -Dark Fairy Tale

(ROMANCE) ROSEWIND BOOKS (Publisher)

When the Wind Chimes
The Seashell of 'Ohana

ROMANCE-NOVELLA
Always Be My Baby

The Crossroads Saga
Crossroads
Between
Beyond
Eternity
Halo City (Novella)

Secret Knights Series (Crossroads spin-off)
The Angel Knights (Novella)
The Chosen Knights
The Blessed Knights
The Sacred Knights
Snow Queen

Descendant Prophecies Series
From Gods
From Deities
From Origins

HALO CITY

From Titans

Watcher Series
Book of Watchers
Book of Enchantresses

High Fantasy
Once Upon a Legend
Once Upon A Kingdom

Crown of Wings and Thorns

BOOKS BY M. CLARKE (Pen Name)

Something Great Series
Something Real (Novella)
Something Great
Something Wonderful
Something Forever
Something Amazing
Something Precious
Twas The Knight Before Christmas (Novella)

Knight Fashion Series
Sexiest Man Alive
Sexiest Couple Alive
Sexiest Dad Alive

My Clarity Series
My Clarity
My Serenity

Behind The Door Written with Alexandrea Weis

About the Author

Born in Seoul, Korea, author Mary Ting is an international bestselling, multi-gold award winning author. Her books span a wide range of genres, and her storytelling talents have earned a devoted legion of fans, as well as garnered critical praise. She is a diverse voice who writes diverse characters, often dealing with a catastrophic world.

Becoming an author happened by chance. It was a way to grieve the death of her beloved grandmother and inspired by a dream she had in high school. After realizing she wanted to become a full-time author, Mary retired from teaching. She also had the privilege of touring with the Magic Johnson Foundation to promote literacy and her children's chapter book: No Bullies Allowed.

Website: www.authormaryting.com
BookBub: https://www.bookbub.com/profile/mary-ting
News Update: http://eepurl.com/iuKvMw
Group page: https://bit.ly/3tyVy0q
Facebook: https://www.facebook.com/AuthorMaryTing
Instagram: http://instagram.com/authormaryting
TikTok: https://www.tiktok.com/@marytingauthor
Twitter: @MaryTing https://twitter.com/MaryTing
Email: authormaryting@outlook.com

Made in the USA
Middletown, DE
22 January 2024

47716606R00064